Benjamin West and His Cat Grimalkin

Benjamin West

AND HIS CAT
GRIMALKIN

By
MARGUERITE HENRY
and
WESLEY DENNIS

MACMILLAN PUBLISHING COMPANY
NEW YORK
COLLIER MACMILLAN PUBLISHERS
LONDON

Macmillan Publishing Company
866 Third Avenue, New York, NY 10022
Collier Macmillan Canada, Inc.

Originally published by The Bobbs-Merrill Company in 1947; reissued by Macmillan in 1987.
Printed in the United States of America
10 9 8 7 6 5 4 3 2 1

Library of Congress Cataloging-in-Publication Data
Henry, Marguerite, date.
  Benjamin West and his cat Grimalkin.
  Summary: With his beloved black cat Grimalkin as his constant companion, the young Quaker boy Benjamin West discovers and develops his talent as an artist.
    1. West, Benjamin, 1738-1820—Juvenile fiction. [1. West, Benjamin 1738-1820—Fiction. 2. Artists—Fiction. 3. Quakers—Fiction. 4. Cats—Fiction] I. Dennis, Wesley. II. Title.
PZ7.H394Be 1987   [Fic]   86-28658
ISBN 0-02-743660-8

TO MY BROTHERS AND SISTERS

THIS is the story of the Quaker lad, Benjamin West, and his cat, Grimalkin, who lived in the wilds of America when Pennsylvania was still a province, and the Indians were saying, "*Itah! Good* be to you!"

Because Quakers thought that pictures were needless, Benjamin never saw a picture; that is, not until he grew up to be seven years old and painted one himself.

Some people say it was the Delaware Indians who helped Benjamin to fame and fortune. Some say it was an artist and seaman by the name of William Williams. And some insist that it was Uncle Phineas Pennington, a merchant of Philadelphia.

But if Benjamin himself could have settled the question, he would probably have said:

"Why, it was Grimalkin, my glossy black cat with the uncommonly long tail!"

As for Grimalkin, he would have pricked his ears forward with pleasure and purred in agreement. For while *he* did not go to

London to visit the Queen, he helped send Benjamin there to visit the King. And it wasn't long before Benjamin West was Court Painter to King George III and had a fine studio right in his palace.

When artists in America heard about Benjamin's good fortune, they came knocking at his door. There were John Copley, Charles Wilson Peale, Gilbert Stuart, John Trumbull, Thomas Sully and more besides. Benjamin West helped them all because he remembered when he was a boy and needed help.

Today Benjamin West is remembered because he was the father of American painting; and many like to think of him as the only American ever to become President of the Royal Academy of England. But I like to remember him as a boy who wanted so very much to paint that he dug his colors out of the earth and made his brushes from his cat's tail.

MARGUERITE HENRY

Contents

Benjamin West and His Cat Grimalkin

1. Welcome to Door-Latch Inn

BENJAMIN woke with a jerk. He held his breath, trying to separate the sounds that came floating up from the innyard. Usually he slept through noises. Travelers could lift the latch, help themselves to the snack of food set out for them, warm themselves by the fire, and leave without his so much as hearing them. But tonight there was a small sound that he could not make out.

In a moment everything went quiet. Papa's hound dogs stopped yapping. The rumble of cart wheels died. It was like the stillness that often comes in the middle of a storm.

Benjamin raised himself up on one elbow. He wished he had ears like a horse so that he could swivel them around to catch the tiniest sound. There! The little noise came again. It was not the trembling cry of a screech owl. It was not the creaking of the inn signboard, or the frightening howl of a wolf. It sounded more like a boy.

13

In a flash Benjamin's bare feet were on the stool that acted as a mounting block for his high bed. Soundlessly he dropped to the floor and hurried over to the tiny square window.

He threw open the shutters and poked his head out into the frosty November night.

The courtyard, spread out below him, was washed in moonlight. He could see a man leading two scrawny oxen to the shed. He could make out the figures of a woman and a boy on the seat of the oxcart.

Suddenly the boy bent over something in his lap and let out a dry sob.

Benjamin tore off his nightshirt. His clothes lay heaped on a bench in a white patch of moonlight. Quickly he slipped into his leather jerkin and knee breeches. How cold they felt! Perhaps the boy was crying because he was cold. But no, figured Benjamin, as he pulled on his hand-knit stockings and hobnail shoes, it took more than cold to make a boy cry like that.

Shivering, he lifted the latch and tiptoed out into the hall.

"Papa!" he cried, as he collided with Mr. West, who was walking briskly toward him with a candle in his hand. Benjamin tried to straighten the candle which he had tipped at a crazy angle. He daubed at the hot tallow which had spilled down Mr. West's coat.

Then he looked up at his father and, frightened as he was, he wanted to laugh. In the long shadows made by the candle, his father looked exactly like the scarecrow in Mamma's kitchen garden. The scarecrow wore a sober Quaker jacket and a white nightcap to frighten the crows. And here was Mr. West dressed like the sober Quaker he was, except for a white nightcap perched on his head.

But even with his nightcap on, Papa looked forbidding.

"Benjamin!" he said, his eyebrows scowling. "Must thee meet every guest?"

"No, Papa," replied Benjamin earnestly, "but there is a boy crying. A *grown* boy of seven or eight like me."

Papa pulled off his nightcap and tucked it in his pocket. "Come along then," he said. "Step sprightly. I may need thee."

Benjamin followed the black coattails of his father as they flapped down the narrow, winding stairway.

At the foot of the stairs Mr. West lighted the lanthorn that hung on an iron hook. Then he pinched out his candle, and set it on the candle shelf.

Benjamin cast a quick glance around the kitchen. Two Indians lay wrapped in blankets on the floor, their feet to the fire. They grunted in their sleep, then drew their heads into their blankets, like turtles drawing into their shells.

Benjamin and his father singled out their own black hats from the long row that hung on pegs near the door. Then they went out into the night.

In the bright moonlight they saw the boy seated on the upping block used in mounting horses. His parents hovered over him like anxious birds.

"Welcome to Door-Latch Inn in the County of Chester in the Province of Pennsylvania!" spoke Papa in a voice so big it rattled the windows.

The little family started at the sound.

"I am John West, innkeeper," Papa said as he held the lanthorn high. "And this is my youngest-born, Benjamin."

"So?" said the stranger, shaking hands stiffly. "And I am Johann Ditzler. By me iss my wife and my little feller, Jacob. We come over the seas from the Rhineland. By morning early we make the journey west. Over the mountains we find good land."

Papa nodded. Then he pointed to the boy who sat on the upping block, rocking back and forth, holding something tightly in his arms.

"What," asked Papa, "ails thy boy?"

"Ach," replied Mr. Ditzler, "such troubles we got! Jacob,

here, he got a sick kitten. We want he should leave it go, but he cries his eyes out. Tch, tch!"

"Ya," spoke up Mrs. Ditzler. "By Philadelphia it makes down rain. Our big cat and her kitten got all spritzed. Our big cat she dies on us. Soon, now, we lose her kitten. And Jacob iss crying. Chust listen! Such a big boy he iss, too."

Jacob turned to Benjamin for help. In an instant, Benjamin was on his knees, peering into Jacob's arms. And there, lying limp and motionless, was a tiny black kitten. Benjamin listened to its harsh breathing. Then he felt the kitten's nose. "As hot as an ember," he whispered to Jacob.

Benjamin longed to tug at his father's coattails. What kind of way was this to save a sick kitten? Why did grownups waste so much time in talk?

"Animals," Papa was saying, as his breath made little white clouds of steam, "are creatures of God. They need protection in suffering."

The German parents were too tired and cold to do any more talking. All they wanted was a place to lay their heads.

Benjamin could stand the delay no longer.

"Please, Papa!" he whispered. "Elmira, the barn cat, has kittens. Six of them."

He spoke quickly now for fear Papa would not listen to his plan. "She will scarce notice one more."

Papa blinked up at the moon. He frowned. For a long moment he stroked his chin. At last he handed Benjamin the lanthorn. "Thee may try," he said. "Dr. Moris says a mother cat will oft adopt a hungry kitten. But warm a jug of milk, first. Mayhap the kitten will not need a foster mother."

Benjamin's heart leaped. He suddenly felt as important as

Dr. Moris. He could almost feel Dr. Moris' big red bush wig upon his head. But he was glad he was still a boy. He could run!

He ran now across the courtyard and the barnyard, around the worn path to the cellar. He lifted the heavy trap door and clattered down the cobblestone steps, his lanthorn making long shadows on the wall. He made his way past barrels of sweet-smelling apples without even stopping to fill his pockets.

The milk crock was full. The good yellow cream had risen to the top. Carefully he ladled it into a tiny jug. Then he hurried into the kitchen. It was bright with firelight now, and a kettle was singing over the fire.

Mamma was up, pouring hot water into the teapot, spreading rye-an'-Injun bread with rich brown apple butter, saying a quiet word to comfort the little German family, who sat in a row on the hooded settle.

Benjamin glanced at the kitten. It was still breathing. He placed the jug of cream in a little nook in the chimney. "It will soon be warm," he said to Jacob, and smiled a little smile of encouragement. Then he took the rush basket used for gathering eggs and in no time at all he was in the barn, reaching into the haymow for Elmira and one of her kittens.

Elmira struggled, but Benjamin held her and her kitten firmly in the basket. All the while he talked in a soft voice.

"I'll bring thee back to the rest of thy family soon," he promised. Then he hurried back to the inn, balancing the basket as carefully as if it held new-laid eggs.

"See!" whispered Benjamin to Jacob as he stroked the big mother cat. "This be Elmira. She will mother thy kitten too. Please to put it in the basket."

Gently the boy laid his kitten alongside Elmira's kitten. Then

Benjamin set the basket on the floor close to the warmth of the fire.

The room turned quiet. All eyes were on the basket. Not a word was said. Only the fire whistled up the chimney, and the Indians grunted in their sleep.

For two or three seconds the barn cat stared at the strange kitten. Then she sniffed it curiously. Her nose wrinkled. The fur flew up on her back. Her tail stiffened. *"P-h-h-f-t! Sp-f-f-t!"* she spat at him. Suddenly, she turned to her own kitten and began washing its face.

Benjamin said a quick prayer under his breath. Please, God, make Elmira be a mother to the sick kitten. Then in case his prayer might not be answered at once he tiptoed around the chimney and reached up for the jug of cream.

"Benjamin!" commanded Mr. West. "Take Elmira back to the barn. Thy plan will not work."

Benjamin was so startled at hearing his father's voice that he upset the jug.

"Oh!" cried Benjamin.

And "Ach!" echoed Jacob as the cream spilled over into the basket, right on top of his kitten.

Now it so happened that Elmira had been raised on skimmed milk. And when she saw the thick yellow cream dripping into the basket, she began licking it from the black kitten's coat.

Up and down went Elmira's head as her pink tongue licked every bit of the rich cream from the kitten's back. And then the strangest thing happened. When all the cream was gone, she kept right on licking. She kept right on stroking the sick kitten with her rough, warm tongue.

Benjamin glanced sidelong at the boy. He laughed out for joy.

Papa clicked his tongue in amazement.

The kitten was stirring ever so slightly. He was stretching! He was letting out a hungry mewing sound.

"Oh!" breathed Benjamin.

"Ach!" sighed Jacob.

Now Elmira was lying on her side, nosing the black kitten and wriggling up to him. After what seemed a long time, but actually was only a matter of seconds, the black kitten began to nuzzle along the barn cat's belly. And at last he and the white kitten were nursing side by side!

A good feeling came over the whole room. Elmira purred until she sounded like a spinning wheel. Then she looked up at the anxious watchers with a pleased smirk on her face.

"Ach, na," clucked Mrs. Ditzler, "everything gets all right!"

"Ai yai yai!" choked Mr. Ditzler as he patted Jacob on the head.

Even Papa seemed happy. He blew his nose as loud as a trumpet.

2. A Wish I Make

THE first finger of light found Benjamin's bed. He turned his face to the wall, enjoying that delicious moment half-awake, half-asleep. He sank deep into his feather bed. He pretended it was a great white cloud floating in the sky.

Suddenly he felt someone in bed beside him. He turned. Why, it was Jacob!

He is tired, thought Benjamin. I shall lie very still. But the harder Benjamin tried to lie still, the more he squirmed. And at last Jacob began to stir, too.

"Is thee awake?" whispered Benjamin.

Jacob sat up startled. Then his face twisted into a shy smile. "Sure," he sighed, as if he were sorry about it. Then he snuggled down under the warm covers. "Benjamin," he whispered, "I make dreams in my sleep."

Benjamin wriggled his toes in excitement. Perhaps if he listened to Jacob's dream, then Jacob would listen to his.

"By Philadelphia," Jacob began, his voice low and full of wonder, "by Philadelphia we see ships building. Soon I am a man. Soon big ships I make. Just like in my dream."

"I believe thee will do it!" Benjamin remarked politely.

Now it was *his* turn. He sat bolt upright in bed. He forgot that he had dozens of chores to do.

"Jacob!" he blurted out. "I dream, too. Even when I am awake."

"Ya?" Jacob asked.

"I dream," said Benjamin very slowly, "I dream how some day I will paint pictures."

"No!" exclaimed Jacob, his voice rising.

"Yes!"

"Pictures," repeated Jacob, as he turned the matter over in his mind. "Like when deer come out from the woods? Like when it makes down rain and sunshine together?"

"Yes, Jacob! That's it! That's it!" Benjamin laughed. He could hardly make his voice sound like his own. At last he had said the words. He had said them right out.

"By mine house we had two pictures," Jacob said proudly.

"Thee did?" asked Benjamin, unbelieving.

"Ya, sure."

"Jacob, I have never seen a picture. I have only heard my Uncle Phineas of Philadelphia tell of them."

"Did you *never* see a picture?"

"No. Never."

"Und why iss it?"

There was a long minute of silence. "We are Quakers," said Benjamin soberly. "Quakers think pictures are needless."

Jacob sobered too. He tried to find words to tell Benjamin how sorry he was. But no words came. Then, suddenly, his eyes brightened. "I make you a present," he said, as if that would fix everything.

Again there was an uncomfortable silence.

"It iss the kitten I give you," Jacob said at last.

"Thy little black kitten?"

"Ya," choked Jacob. "It makes easier to know he iss by you."

"Oh, Jacob! I will take good care of him. He shall be our house cat. Never will he have to live in the barns!"

"It wonders me if the kitten forgets Grimalkin."

"Grimalkin?" repeated Benjamin.

"Ya. Grimalkin was his mother."

"Would thee like to have me name the kitten Grimalkin?"

Jacob seemed to have trouble in answering. Then the bed began to quiver.

Now Benjamin wished *he* could think of something comforting to say. He stole a glance at Jacob.

But Jacob was not crying. He was shaking with laughter.

"Ach, Benjamin," he giggled, "Grimalkin iss a she-cat's name. But the kitten—he don't mind."

"No. Of course not. We'll call him Grimalkin. For his mother."

All of a sudden the inn seemed to come alive. There was the sound of heavy boots in the hall. Horses snorted and whinnied in the courtyard. Voices called back and forth. There were the deep, throaty voices of the Germans. There were the burring voices of the Scotch-Irish. But Papa's stately voice boomed above them all as he gave out duties:

"Samuel, this be the day to sow the marshland with grass seed.

"John, thee will brand the new bullocks today.

"Thee, Thomas, will yoke the hogs so they will not stray.

"Joseph, thee and Benjamin can pry up stones to build a fence along the upland pasture."

But Benjamin was not listening. He was sniffing the air as noisily as Papa's hound dogs. The most tantalizing smells were seeping in under the door—ham and scrapple and eggs frying, pippin apples and cinnamon buns baking, and the steaming fragrance of herb tea.

"Jacob!" shouted Benjamin. "On with thy clothes!"

Both boys leaped out of bed and then burst into laughter. Except for their hats and shoes they were completely dressed.

As Benjamin put on his shoes, he also put on a sober manner. Begin the day in quiet. Do not raise thy voice, he repeated under his breath. This morning Papa will not need to remind me.

Then he promptly forgot his words as he and Jacob tumbled down the stairs and into the bustling activity of the kitchen. Mamma was moving silently and swiftly from fire to table. Benjamin's four sisters seemed everywhere at once—filling the salt and sugar boxes, putting chairs and benches in place. Even Jacob's mother was helping.

"Benjamin!" said Sarah, his oldest sister, "wash thy face at once. Then blow on the conch shell. Breakfast is ready."

Benjamin was so used to Sarah's chatter that he hardly heard her. He and Jacob were over in the chimney corner on their hands and knees. They were peering into the egg basket in awe.

Elmira was still there! And someone had brought in all of her own white kittens. And the black kitten was there, too. He was a smart one, snuggled in among all the white kittens for warmth.

Benjamin looked up and caught Mamma's eye. She smiled first at Benjamin, then at Jacob. "The black kitten will be as strong as any," she said softly. "Now off to the wash bench."

Both boys splashed their faces with cold water. Then they took turns blowing on the conch shell until Mr. West and Benjamin's four brothers came in from the woods and fields, and the guests flocked in from wagon shed and courtyard.

Papa sat down at the head of the table, straight and proud. In true Quaker fashion he kept his hat on. It looked as if it had grown there. He waited patiently while his five sons and his twenty guests sat down to table. Then he nodded his head in pleasure. He liked to see every chair and stool and bench and chest occupied. His blue eyes wandered over the table and lingered a moment on the cinnamon buns. He smiled in approval.

When at last a stillness came over the room, he closed his eyes and folded his hands. For a long time no sound escaped his parted lips.

Benjamin could feel little shivers racing up and down his spine. He hoped his father's voice would tremble and quake until the very roof timbers shook.

"Al-migh-ty God," the trembling began.

At the unexpected quaking sound Jacob jumped and almost fell off his stool.

"Be not frightened," whispered Benjamin; "that is why we are called *Quakers*."

"It is the duty of man," Papa was praying, "to care for all living creatures, large and small. The lowliest creature has a

work to do. The wren protects the fruit of the orchard. The barn cat protects the grain. The house cat protects man's food. We thank Thee, O Lord, for sparing the life of a plain black kitten."

Benjamin opened one eye and looked around the table. His brothers, John, Thomas, Samuel and Joseph, sat thoughtful and grave, their eyes straight ahead, yet seeing nothing. The heads of the guests were bowed low.

Mamma and the girls stood behind the table. They were waiting to pour the tea, to refill the serving dishes.

Of all the people in the room only Benjamin let his eyes wander. He watched the wisps of steam rising from the serving bowls. He could almost taste the flavorsome scrapple on his tongue. And just when he thought he could not wait another moment, Papa began to look natural once more. He spoke to the traveler beside him in his regular voice. It was the signal to eat. Immediately knives and spoons clattered against wooden plates. Meanwhile, over in the rush basket, the kittens squirmed and slept and made small mewing sounds.

All too soon, breakfast was over. Whips cracked. Axles creaked. Oxcarts began rumbling out of the innyard.

Benjamin and Jacob stood over the kittens in an awkward silence.

It was Jacob who spoke first.

"Benjamin," he said.

"Yes?"

"A wish I make. You could paint so fine a picture of Grimalkin that anyone could tell iss a cat you paint."

Benjamin glanced around quickly to see if anyone had heard. Then their eyes locked.

"I make a wish, too," he whispered. "One day in Philadelphia

I will find thee building a great sailship. And I shall set up my easel on the bank. And I shall paint the whole harbor!"

"Jacob! Come! Already we go," his mother called.

Arm in arm Jacob and Benjamin walked slowly out of the inn.

"Good-by, Benjamin," said Jacob with a catch in his voice. "I wish you could go with." He looked back over his shoulder toward the inn. "Good-by, Grimalkin," he said, scarcely above a whisper.

Then he let go of Benjamin's arm and took his place alongside his father. Today he would not climb aboard the wagon. Today he would help lead the oxen. It was as if he had grown into a man overnight.

Slowly the cart rattled out of the courtyard, past the signboard swinging from the buttonwood tree, past the yapping dogs, and off into the wilderness.

Benjamin watched until Jacob and finally the whole cart were swallowed up and lost among the black tree trunks.

Then he kicked the upping block to keep from crying.

3. A Good Fishing Day

THERE was a kind of magic in the way Grimalkin grew. His fur began to fluff out, soft and black and shining. His tail became thick and uncommonly long. His body waxed strong and very nimble.

And it was like magic the way he took possession of Door-Latch Inn. Almost as soon as Elmira and her kittens were returned to the barn, he began to look after things.

Indoors and out, he set his own tasks. If one of the hound dogs so much as showed his nose in the parlor, Grimalkin cuffed him smartly and sent him yammering out the door. If the chickens got into Mamma's kitchen garden, it was Grimalkin who chased them out. He also took care of the ground hogs and rabbits and snakes. There were the mouse holes to watch-too. And the cows to bring in. He not only helped round them up; he also thought

it wise to be on hand during the milking. No matter who did the milking—John or Thomas or Samuel or Joseph, or even Papa—he would squirt some of the fresh milk right into Grimalkin's mouth. Grimalkin had to be there to catch it!

Never was a cat so busy. Nor so independent. He slept where he pleased—on the candle shelf, or in a drawer atop Mamma's newly spun cloth, or on Papa's basket-bottom chair. But if the weather was cold, he liked to toast his bones before the fire or crawl into bed with Benjamin. Often, in the dead of night when the moon was full, he would take it into his head to go hunting. And being as clever as he was independent, he asked no one to let him out. With one paw he could lift the door latch as neatly as if he had four fingers and a thumb.

In no time at all Grimalkin was everyone's pet. Papa and Benjamin's four brothers liked him because he was a great ratter and mouser. Mamma and Benjamin's four sisters liked him because, as Mamma so often said, "A more mannerly cat thee would not find anywhere. What other cat in all the Province wipes his paws on the doormat before entering the kitchen? Polite and tidy!" she added with a bright nod.

Even Nanny Luddy, Papa's big mare, liked Grimalkin. She would sleep standing if Grimalkin chose to lie on her bed of straw. Yet Grimalkin treated Nanny Luddy as if he were a king and she his slave. If he leaped upon her back to warm his paws, one would have thought, by the airs he put on, that he was doing her quite a favor.

As for the guests who came and went, Grimalkin openly disapproved them. After investigating them with his nose he left them strictly alone. And when their carts rattled out of the inn-yard, he helped chase them on their way and then flew back to

the inn as if to say, "At last! At last! I have The Family all to myself!"

But if he felt this way toward The Family, he treated Benjamin almost as if he knew that Benjamin had saved his life.

There was nothing he would not do for Benjamin. He would jump through a barrel hoop for him. He would roll over when told. He would box. He would play hide and seek, and a fairly good game of catch and toss. But, more than all this, he was a partner in everything that Benjamin did. And such an understanding grew up between them that strangers would remark on it. "I vow and declare!" they would say. "Grimalkin's tail twitches with excitement and he begins purring at the mere sound of Benjamin's voice."

What these strangers did not know was that Benjamin and Grimalkin could talk to each other almost as person with person. Grimalkin would prick his ears forward and listen gravely to each word of Benjamin's. Then he would make eager little mewing replies, his talk growing louder and louder until he felt certain that Benjamin understood.

There was the day that Benjamin and Grimalkin were left alone to mind Sally. Sally was Benjamin's baby niece.

It was a day made for fishing. Sky overcast. Winds gentle. For a whole hour Benjamin had been sharpening a long pole. He was going to try spearing for trout the way his friends the Indians did.

He had already promised Grimalkin a fishing trip, with all the minnows he could eat.

But just as Benjamin was tucking an apple and some johnny-cake into his shirt, he heard the *cloppety-clop* of a horse's hoofs. And then such a hubbub! Rachel, Benjamin's married sister, came flouncing into the house, carrying baby Sally.

"Oh, Mamma!" she cried. "I have been homesick for thee and Benjamin—and everyone."

Benjamin tried hard to look pleased, but in his mind's eye he saw a trout jump out of the water with a silver splash.

Mamma made little cooing noises to the baby. Then she hung Rachel's hood and cloak on a peg as if she were company.

"Benjamin!" she said. "Run up to the front bedchamber and fetch down the cradle we let the little Scotch baby sleep in last night."

With Grimalkin at his heels, Benjamin took the stairs two at a time. He returned breathless with a basket which looked like a great bird's nest on rockers. Grimalkin sat inside it, looking enormously pleased with himself.

"Come, Grimalkin," whispered Benjamin, as he set the cradle down and began edging toward the door.

"Thee, Benjamin!" called Mamma. "Please to fetch thy sisters. They will want to see our dear Sally."

"Where are they, Mamma?" asked Benjamin in despair.

"They are gathering wild mint by the creek!"

"Oh, Benjamin," cried Rachel in her most pleading manner, "I long to be out there with them. If thee were to mind Sally, Mamma and I could have a little outing."

Benjamin bit his lips. He did not mind fetching wood or water. He did not even mind cleaning out the hen house—very much. But minding the baby on a good fishing day!

At a sharp look from Mamma, however, he sat down quickly.

"Oh, thank thee, brother," smiled Rachel. "Here is the fly-trap. Please to keep the flies away from Sally's face."

Before Benjamin could say a word, he found himself face to face with the wailing Sally.

"Why, she's mostly mouth!" he said with disgust.

Grimalkin's ears were thrown backward in disapproval. "Can't thee *do* something about this noise?" he seemed to ask.

"Why, of course, I can," replied Benjamin. "I can rock the cradle."

The wailing stopped at once.

The room grew so quiet that Benjamin fancied he could hear the bread rising.

The minutes seemed like hours. The day was going to waste! Benjamin kept tiptoeing to the door to watch for Mamma and Rachel.

"Poor Grimalkin," he sighed, "I promised thee some minnows. And here we are, caught like insects in a web."

He looked about the room. Suddenly his eyes fell on the wells of red ink and black ink on Papa's counter. Beside them lay a goose-quill pen, a sand box for blotting the ink, and a fresh sheet of paper. How smooth and clean the paper looks! thought Benjamin. Then he turned to see if the flies were bothering Sally. And at that precise moment, the baby happened to smile in her sleep.

"Why, Grimalkin!" Benjamin cried. "Sally is less funny-looking when she smiles. She is quite fair." His fingers reached for the goose-quill pen. "I could draw her picture!" he said in amazement. "I believe I could!"

Grimalkin smoothed his whiskers against Benjamin's leg. Then he gazed up with mischievous green eyes. "Well, why doesn't thee do it?" he purred, as plainly as words. "Who is to stop thee?"

4. Only a Piece of Paper

BENJAMIN had to work rapidly. Sally's pleasant dream would not last forever. Besides, Mamma and the girls might walk in any minute.

He placed the clean sheet of paper and Papa's ink wells and sand box on a bench beside the cradle. He knelt down on the floor. He dipped the goose-quill pen into the black ink.

Scratch! Scratch! went the pen. With quick strokes he sketched the outline of Sally's head. Then, very lightly, he drew her features. The faint eyebrows. The closed lids. The rounded nose. The smiling lips.

His eyes darted back and forth from Sally's face to his drawing. He forgot about the spear he had made. He forgot about the beautiful red-bellied trout. He forgot everything in the excitement of making his first sketch.

There! He could try the red ink now. He wiped the pen in his hair as he had seen the travelers do. Then he dipped it in the red ink and gave Sally an orange-red mouth. With round-and-round lines he sketched her silken curls. "Why, the color nigh matches her own!" he exclaimed.

Just then Grimalkin leaped on his shoulder and patted his cheek with a gentle forepaw.

"Can thee see any likeness to our Sally?" Benjamin asked of him.

Grimalkin seemed to gaze fixedly at the picture. Then he opened his wide pink mouth. "*Mrr-aow,*" he said, in complete approval.

Benjamin laughed out for joy. But his laughter was cut short. There, in the doorway, stood Mamma and Rachel and Sarah and Hannah and Mary and Elizabeth.

Benjamin sprang to his feet, upsetting the sand box, and almost upsetting the ink wells. He hid his drawing behind him. He could almost hear Mamma say: "If the world's people wish to draw, well and good. But *thee* is a Quaker, son. Thy grandfather was chief councilor for William Penn himself!"

Mamma stood rigid, holding bunches of bright green mint in her hands. Behind her clustered the girls, their eyes questioning.

At last Mamma came toward Benjamin with slow, measured steps.

"Benjamin!" she said crisply.

"Y-y-yes, Mamma."

"What is thee hiding?"

"Only a piece of paper, Mamma."

"I would see it."

Benjamin winced. He handed her the picture and waited for

the shocked, hurt look to cross her face. He watched Rachel and
Sarah and Hannah and Mary and Elizabeth gather around the
picture. He heard their little gasps of surprise.

Then something happened which Benjamin did not in the
least expect. Mamma clapped her hand over her mouth as if to
smother an outcry of pleasure. Her eyes grew big with wonder.

"Why, 'tis our Sally!" she exclaimed. "An excellent likeness of our dear Sally." And then she smiled down at Benjamin. "How would thee and Grimalkin like to go fishing now?" she asked. "Papa ever was fond of fresh trout. But what he will say to picture-making, I do not know."

Benjamin's face grew as red as a coxcomb. Why, Mamma had not minded at all!

"What did I tell thee?" Grimalkin seemed to say as he reared up on his hind legs and put his forepaws into Benjamin's hand.

Benjamin's heart danced. He picked up his spear, his apples and his johnnycake, and turned to go.

"We'll be back in time to bring home the cows," he sang out.

Grimalkin lifted the latch, and together the boy and the cat set off across the innyard.

"Oh-ho!" laughed Benjamin. "Thy tail is a weather vane, Grimalkin. It stands straight as a poker whenever thee is happy."

Grimalkin led the way, and the sound of his purring was like the gladness in Benjamin's heart.

5. The Image of Sally

WEEKS went by before Papa saw the picture of Sally. By day he was busy planting Indian corn and pumpkins. By night the guests hovered around him like bees after honey. They hung on his every word, for while Papa was a man of few words, each one counted.

By the time he had a moment to spare, there was not only the picture of Sally to show him. There was a whole stack of pictures, done on poplar boards, on birch bark—on *anything* that would hold a pen stroke or a smudge of charcoal.

It was midmorning of a bright May day when Papa first heard about the pictures.

"Benjamin!" he called out as he came into the kitchen, bringing the smell of rich black earth with him. "Nanny Luddy has lost a shoe. See if the smith can attend her at once."

"Oh, yes, Papa," replied Benjamin quickly. He grinned at the thought that now Sarah or Hannah or Mary or Elizabeth would have to come down from her bedmaking and take over his job. He was doing a hot and tiresome chore at the time. He was sitting on the hearthstone, turning the crank handle that turned a joint of meat before the fire. And every now and then he had to baste the meat with the brown gravy that dripped into the pan beneath.

Grimalkin sat watchful at Benjamin's feet. Memory told him that sometimes the gravy spattered on the hearthstone, and all of the spatters belonged to him.

"The sun has great power this morning," Papa remarked. "It is pleasant and cool inside."

Cool! thought Benjamin as he wiped the beads of perspiration from his upper lip.

Papa sat down at the table. He began sampling the wild strawberries that Mamma was putting in a pie. Then, looking as sheepish as a boy, he reached over and scooped up on one finger some of the floating island pudding that stood cooling in a bowl. He smiled up at Mamma. "The pudding is exactly to my taste," he observed.

"Benjamin," said Mamma, "this would be the time to show Papa thy pictures."

At the word *picture* Papa coughed and sat bolt upright. His hands tightened on his whip handle until the knuckles stood out white and big. His face went redder than the strawberries. He fixed his hat more firmly on his head.

Oh, oh! thought Benjamin. How quickly Papa can change!

Grimalkin rolled over and over to attract attention, but Papa took less notice of him than if he had been a fly.

"Ho, ho! Look at Grimalkin!" laughed Benjamin nervously.

A heavy silence was the only answer.

Slowly Benjamin got up and walked over to the pine dresser. If only John or Thomas or Samuel or Joseph would come to get Papa! But Door-Latch Inn was as still as a meetinghouse. Only the hens clucked beneath the windows.

With trembling hands, Benjamin took the stack of pictures from the bottom drawer of the dresser. He handed Papa the one of Sally.

It was as if Papa hated even to touch it. Gingerly he laid it on his lap. He reached into his pocket and took out his square-rimmed spectacles. Slowly he adjusted them under his beetling brows. Then he brought the picture up close.

For a long moment he said nothing. Grimalkin lowered his tail at the awful stillness. Mamma's spoon dropped out of her hand with a loud clatter.

Finally Papa placed the drawing on the table. "The image of Sally should be carried in our hearts," he said, as he looked up over the rims of his spectacles. "Not on a piece of paper. Pictures fade; memories remain green forever."

"Green!" shouted Benjamin. "How I long to put green into my pictures! I tried to draw a hummer bird yesterday, as he dipped his beak into a flower. I wanted to paint his shiny green head. But all I had was red and black ink."

Papa shook his head, as he looked at the pictures of redheaded

woodpeckers and swamp roses and bushes with scarlet berries

"It would be better to study cabbages and turnips. Or even gooseberries," he said with a sniff. "These are gay and gaudy. Pride in pictures shows a worldly spirit."

"But, Papa! I am *not* proud of these pictures. I aim to do better. Much better. If only I had more colors!"

At this Papa gave up. "Tell me why it is that thee must draw?" he asked.

Now Benjamin was at a loss. How could he explain the need for putting things on paper? How could he explain that?

"Was it that Sally's smile is fleeting and thee wished to hold it?" asked Mamma.

"That's it, Mamma. That's it! The hummer bird, too, is gone in winter. Yet I could capture him on paper."

Now Grimalkin stretched his muscles and looked up at Papa as if he wished to add a few remarks. First he uttered a little sneeze to attract attention, as people sometimes clear their throats Then he started talking.

"*Yee-oo, mrr-aow, mee-aw-oo, ye-ah-oo.*" Louder and louder he talked until finally he flung back his head and opened his mouth so wide it showed all the black ridges inside.

Papa sat silent and thoughtful for a moment. Then his eyes twinkled. "Grimalkin is right," he said. "To preserve *good* actions on paper can do no harm. Benjamin is but a lad, Mamma. He will outgrow this." Then turning to Benjamin he said, "Thee may continue with thy drawing—*if* it does not interfere with chores."

Benjamin wanted to scoop Grimalkin up in his arms and dance in circles like a whirl beetle. He wanted to toss Papa's hat to the sky. He wanted to hug Papa until they both gasped for breath. But all he said was, "Thank thee, Papa. Now I shall see about Nanny Luddy's shoe." And he frisked Grimalkin's whiskers for pure joy.

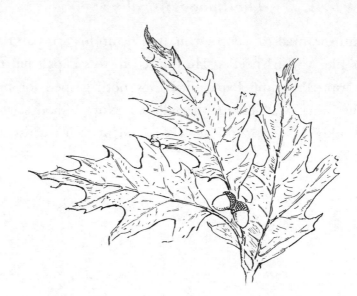

6. A-Leafing

"THERE!" exclaimed Papa the next morning as he swung a sack of corn on Nanny Luddy's back. "Hop up in front of the sack and sit firm, Benjamin. Thee is a great stout lad of seven."

"I am rising eight, Papa," corrected Benjamin.

"By my life!" chuckled Papa. "*Time* thee was taking the corn to Miller Clinkenbeard's for grinding. Thy brother Samuel is needed in the fields."

Grimalkin came streaking across the courtyard and leaped up on the sack of corn, his paws clinging to Benjamin's coat.

At first Benjamin felt big and important to take over Samuel's work. But it turned out to be a great disappointment. Miller Clinkenbeard did not take his customers in turn. He ground the grain for the grownups first. Sometimes Benjamin had to wait for hours. To make matters worse, the miller treated him like a baby—chucking him under the chin, ruffling his hair and teasing him about needing a cat for company. And when it came time to go, he would actually try to lift Benjamin and Grimalkin, too, onto Nanny Luddy's back.

Grimalkin sometimes laid back his ears and scratched at the miller.

"Please, sir," Benjamin would say, "Grimalkin and I can mount Nanny by ourselves. If thee will hoist the sack of meal across her back, we can be off."

All the way home Benjamin's face would smart at the memory of Miller Clinkenbeard's laughter.

As time went by, Benjamin's chores doubled. There never seemed a moment left for drawing. Once he had eagerly sanded down some poplar boards and was all ready to draw the weather-vane horse on the barn when along came Papa. At sight of the drawing boards he squinted his eyes and pursed his lips. Then suddenly his face lighted.

"Benjamin!" he exclaimed. "Has thee noted how the sheep are leaving their wool on bushes and weeds? I would have thee pluck these bits of fleece and put them in a sack. Only watch against the ram that he does not butt thee or Grimalkin."

"Yes, Papa," sighed Benjamin as he took the sack that Papa offered.

There was no penfold for the sheep. They browsed far and

wide. And wherever they went they left behind their telltale bits of fleece. Benjamin had to spend a whole morning collecting a small sack of wool.

Meanwhile his fingers ached to draw. "I declare!" he complained to Grimalkin. "I would like to exchange places with thee!"

Grimalkin at the time was rocking on his hind feet and slapping at a piece of fleece that had been lifted by the wind. He forgot his play at sound of Benjamin's voice and came over to lick his hand as cats will.

"Someday," Benjamin promised him, "I shall do a fine portrait of thee, Grimalkin. Someday when I have green color to match thy eyes. And someday when I have time!" he added grimly.

From sunup to sundown, he worked. The truth of the matter was that in all the Province of Pennsylvania no lad was kept busier. Up at five—cleaning the hen house, bringing in wood, drawing water from the well, feeding the chickens, gathering eggs, pulling weeds in Mamma's kitchen garden, cleaning out ashes in the fireplace, taking pitchers of warm water and fresh towels to the travelers' rooms.

And once these chores were done, Papa's mind seemed to buzz

with new duties. "Benjamin! It would please Mamma to have a new butter paddle. Whittling is a fine activity. It gives the mind time to think on God." Or, "Benjamin! We sorely need a birdhouse to attract the martins. Foxes have been carrying off our chickens. If we had martins now, they would send out an alarm note to warn the chickens."

And Benjamin would spend hours making a birdhouse for the martins or a butter paddle for Mamma.

"I shall be *glad* to go to school!" Benjamin told Grimalkin fiercely. "I can draw in my copybooks then. And I shall be glad when the days grow shorter. I can draw at night by candlelight."

But Benjamin was wrong. There was no time in school for drawing. Schoolmaster Snevely had a sharp eye for ornament. "Copybooks need no decoration!" he said, tapping his birch rod on Benjamin's knuckles.

Even at candlelighting time the work did not let up. Papa could think up indoor tasks as quickly as outdoor ones.

It was: "Here, lad, thee can whittle some treenails for me." Or, "Here, Benjamin, this be a good time to polish pewter for Mamma, or to crush herbs in the wooden mortar, or to string slices of apple for drying."

One moon-white night Benjamin took a poplar board to bed with him, thinking to draw a silhouette of Grimalkin against the moon. But he awoke at dawn to find his arms locked about the board. He had been too exhausted for anything but sleep.

At the wash bench the next morning Samuel eyed Benjamin and then burst into a great roar of laughter. "Oh, ho! Thy face is growing as long as Nanny Luddy's," he bellowed. "Thee should be over at the horse trough instead of the wash bench."

This was more than Benjamin could bear. And just when things looked their very blackest, suddenly everything brightened. That very morning when Benjamin arrived at school the children were huddled about a sign tacked on the door. The sign read:

*It pains me to be abroad on business for the day. Do not
tarry. Return to your homes at once. Come tomorrow—sharp
at eight.*

                                    Silas Snevely
                                    Schoolmaster

If it pained Schoolmaster Snevely to be away, it did not pain
the children at all. In spite of their Quaker training, they
whooped and shouted. Many of them stayed to play fox and
geese in the schoolyard. But Benjamin raced home.

"Mamma!" he cried. "Master Snevely is away. The school door
is barred. Please, may Grimalkin and I go off into the forest?"

Mamma was busy dipping the girls' caps and neckerchiefs into
a kettle of starch and indigo blue. She straightened up and turned
a searching look on Benjamin.

"With thy drawing boards?" she questioned.

Benjamin nodded.

" 'Thee may continue with thy drawing,' " said Mamma softly,
" 'if it does not interfere with chores.' Those were Papa's words.
I remember them well. Yes, son. Thee may go. And I shall fix
a packet of lunch for thee and some bonny clabber for Grimalkin."

Benjamin leaped into the air. He picked up Grimalkin and
set him on his head like a coonskin cap.

"But what if Papa finds me in the woods and thinks up a
chore?" he asked suddenly, peering out from under Grimalkin's
furry body.

"*I* have already thought of a chore," replied Mamma.

Benjamin bit his lips. Not Mamma! he thought bitterly. Not
Mamma, too!

Mamma went on with her starching. "It is a fine day to go a-leafing," she said. "I need a goodly supply of oak leaves to line the oven floor when I bake my bread. A whole winter's supply I need. Take the stick by the door and string it thick with leaves."

There was a smile between them. Going a-leafing was no chore. None at all. The woods were wild with leaves. In a twinkling he could string the stick. Then the day would be his. *His!*

He could hardly wait for Mamma to slice the rye-an'-Injun bread and the cold ham left over from yesterday's dinner. Then while she wrapped the bonny clabber in a cabbage leaf and flavored a little jug of ciderkin with molasses and ginger, Benjamin made his own plans. He filled his pockets with charcoal. He took a small rough board from the pine dresser, and began sanding it frantically. He kept one eye on the door. Papa and the boys were in the flax patch. "And may they stay there!" he prayed as he rubbed and rubbed.

At last he was ready! With his poplar board and his lunch bulging in his knapsack, he and Grimalkin went out.

The world was red and gold with autumn. Benjamin took a deep breath, as if to inhale his freedom in one gulp. Then he cleared the wash bench in a flying leap.

As he crossed the kitchen garden he looked up at the scarecrow. "Do not expect us at noontide," he said, as he shook the empty tattered sleeve. Then he grinned at his own foolishness.

The road in front of the inn was deserted. There was not a horse or traveler in sight—only a sow and her pink family.

"How does thee do, Friend Sow?" asked Benjamin in passing.

"What's that? Thee would like to have thy picture drawn? It vexes me sorely to disappoint thee. But Grimalkin and I are going a-leafing," he laughed out.

The road was lined on either side with red sumac. Benjamin parted the bushes and found a narrow Indian trail. And just that quickly he and Grimalkin had entered the forest.

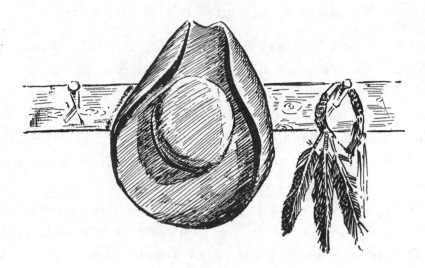

7. "Little Quekel Friends"

How still it was! Benjamin stopped a moment to listen to the
stillness. And then he found that it was not still at all. A hazel-
nut dropped with a thud at his feet. Bird wings whistled through
the forest. And in the distance there was the crackling sound of
fire. Benjamin sniffed the wind and followed his nose in great
excitement.

"The Indians! They must be firing the forest to kill off the
brush," he cried. "Make haste, Grimalkin!"

Grimalkin had stopped to sharpen his claws on a tree. He finished the job to his full satisfaction, then bounded after Benjamin.

Little banners of smoke now came winding around the tree
trunks like ribbons on a Maypole. Benjamin broke into a run.

"I hope it is old Sassoonan!" he panted as he ran. "If it is, he
will bake fish for thee, Grimalkin, and corn cakes for me."

Suddenly Benjamin burst full upon the Indians. The splendor of the sight held him motionless. A great circle of fire was licking at the base of a white fir tree. And around the tree danced Chief Sassoonan and his three sons, Bear and Elk and Beaver. Each waved long poles with moistened rags tied at the ends. Then, as soon as the fire leaped above a certain line on the tree trunk, they snuffed it out with the wet rags. There was a loud hissing sound as the water quenched the fire.

"Why, I know what they are doing!" exclaimed Benjamin. "They are going to fell the tree and hollow out a bark boat!"

The Indians had not heard. They were too close to the crackling of the fire and the hissing of the water.

With quick inspiration Benjamin squatted down on the earth and began sketching the scene on his poplar board. As the Indian figures took shape, he frowned. "I long to paint them a good copper-brown," he said to Grimalkin, who lay curled in the crotch of a tree just above Benjamin's head. "It seems as if I'm never content."

Just then the Indians came running toward Benjamin, their voices raised in a shrill cry. And to the crashing and snapping of boughs, the fir tree toppled to earth.

Grimalkin, trembling in fear, leaped onto Benjamin's shoulder.

"Be not afraid, kitling," comforted Benjamin. "All will soon be quiet."

At that precise moment Sassoonan spied the white boy and the black cat. His old face wrinkled with pleasure. He raised his hand in a salute.

"*Itah!*" he said, in a voice that seemed to come from the bottom of a well. "*Itah,* my little Quekel friends."

"And good be to thee, too!" laughed Benjamin, jumping to his feet.

Then, solemnly, the old Indian chief and the Quaker lad shook hands. Grimalkin sniffed the chief with approval. He liked the smell of bear's grease which clung to him.

Meanwhile Bear and Elk and Beaver had gathered about the drawing board. Their beady eyes never changed expression. For a long time they stared at the picture. Finally Sassoonan joined them and took the board in his hands. He pointed to the tree that Benjamin had drawn.

"Is good," he said.

"Why, he says 'Good'!" exclaimed Benjamin. "Did thee hear that, Grimalkin? Sassoonan says the tree is good."

"Amen!" nodded Bear and Elk and Beaver.

Again Sassoonan picked up the board. This time he pointed to the Indians dancing around the fire. With a look of displeasure he clenched his right fist and threw out his opened hand as if he were tossing away something very unpleasant.

His sons shouted and said, "Amen!"

Benjamin was puzzled. Had he hurt Sassoonan's feelings?

For answer Sassoonan rose, his old knees cracking like the fire. With his forefinger he motioned Benjamin to pick up his drawing board and follow. Then he reached into a shelter of brush and drew out a deerskin bag filled with bear's grease.

In a single file Benjamin, with Grimalkin on his shoulder, and the three young Indians followed Sassoonan. Silently they wound through the forest gloom.

Benjamin was not in the least afraid. Sassoonan was an old friend. Each year he came to Door-Latch Inn with things to sell—baskets and brooms, venison meat and wild turkey, deerskin, bearskin, beaver and raccoon. Many times Sassoonan's clan had raised their wigwams in Papa's orchard and hobbled their horses in the upland meadows. And once Sassoonan had stayed a whole week at the inn while Papa and Mamma went to the Yearly Meeting in Philadelphia.

Now they were coming out on grassy land close to the stream that skirted the inn. A bridge, made of a single tree trunk, lay across the stream. Sassoonan stooped low. He pointed to the bridge and then to his back. It was plain to see that he wanted to carry Benjamin pickaback, as he used to do when Benjamin was very small.

Benjamin blushed. He was much too big to ride pickaback now, but Sassoonan was chief of the Turtle Clan. It was a great honor to be carried by a chief. Besides, he could not offend Sas-soonan. So with Grimalkin still on his shoulder he climbed onto Sassoonan's back, trying to make himself as light as possible.

Benjamin watched the old chief's feet. They curved around the tree trunk as securely as the claws of a woodpecker. He could hardly wait to try it himself.

When they reached the opposite bank things happened so fast that Benjamin's eyes were everywhere at once. At a word from Sassoonan, Bear began scooping up handfuls of red earth. Beaver began scooping up handfuls of yellow clay. Then with a small stone for a muller and a large flat stone for a grinding slab, Bear and Beaver began to grind the lumps of earth. Elk, meanwhile, was gathering mussel shells.

Beaver finished first. His red earth was powdered very fine. Sassoonan now took a mussel shell from Elk and poured some of the powdered earth into it. Then he mixed it with bear's grease and stirred and stirred until it formed a reddish-brown paste. At last, with a look of triumph, he handed the mixture to Benjamin and pointed to the drawing board.

Benjamin dipped his finger into the color. It trembled a little as he painted the Indian figures a rich coppery red.

"Grimalkin!" he shouted. "At last I have color! Color! Color!"

Grimalkin acted as if he understood. He leaped several times into the air and mewed his approval.

"Amen! Amen! Amen!" the Indians cried.

Suddenly they began stripping pieces of birch bark from a stand of trees near the water. Then they squatted on their heels and began to paint on the bark with the red and yellow colors they had made.

Benjamin watched openmouthed. The Indians were working with fine skill. Sassoonan was painting a turtle because he was chief of the Turtle Clan. The youngest Indian was painting a beaver because his name meant beaver. The second Indian was painting a bear, and the third an elk.

What fascinated Benjamin was the way they laid on their colors. Beaver had chewed the stem of a tall spear of grass and was using the chewed end exactly as if it were a goose-quill pen. Sassoonan was using a flat piece of wood that looked like a miniature butter paddle. And Elk was using a piece of birch bark.

"Think on it!" Benjamin whispered to Grimalkin. "The Indians like to draw, too. At last I've found some *real* schoolfellows." And right there in the heart of Penn's forest Benjamin West joined his first art class.

The sun was directly overhead when the Indians went back to finish their boat. While Grimalkin sunned himself in a small patch of sunlight, Benjamin helped the Indians gather dry twigs

to lay on top of the felled trunk. He helped set fire to them. He even helped swab the sides of the trunk. After the fire had scooped a deep hollow in the trunk, Bear and Elk and Beaver scraped the inside surface with pieces of flint.

Benjamin watched them a long time to see just how it was done. Then he gathered oak leaves until his stick was full.

"Little Quekel friends soon eat!" announced Sassoonan when the inside of the canoe was scraped as smooth as a stone. While corn cakes roasted in the charred tree stump, Bear and Elk and Beaver invited Benjamin to go fishing. With nothing but birds' claws for fish hooks they caught eight sunfish and a red-bellied trout. Grimalkin had good luck, too. He caught a frog.

Afternoon found Benjamin and the Indians sitting on the floor of the forest, sharing their food. How Sassoonan and his sons enjoyed the sliced ham and the fresh bread and ciderkin! They even ate Grimalkin's bonny clabber. As for Benjamin and Grimalkin, they preferred the corn cakes and the fish. They ate until they could hold no more.

Sassoonan grunted contentedly when the meal was over. He took a clay pipe out of the skin pouch that hung around his neck. He filled it with tobacco and puffed slowly. After a long silence he spoke softly to his sons. At once they brought out their bows and arrows and taught Benjamin how to shoot flying squirrels on the wing. Then they showed him how to make a sun sign

They drew a circle on the ground with a sharp stone, and drove a twig into the center of the circle, bending it in the direction of the sun.

"I see!" nodded Benjamin. "If we should be scouts, we could make a sun sign for our followers. It would tell them when we left here."

"Amen!" replied the Indians, pleased at the quickness of their pupil.

Suddenly Benjamin realized that the twig pointed to sunset-time. He picked up his stick of leaves and his poplar board and whistled for Grimalkin.

"Run! Run!" spoke Sassoonan. "Cold night soon here. Good-by, little Quekel friends."

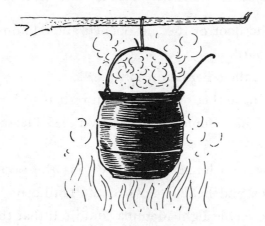

8. A Stick of Indigo Blue

BENJAMIN parted the bushes. He did not cross the road at once. He stood there, looking at the inn. He could see the windows bright with firelight. He could see wood smoke curling from the chimney, brushing the face of the moon. He could see into the horse shed. By the light of the lanthorn that hung over the entrance it looked as if every stall were filled. That meant the inn, too, would be crowded.

Suddenly Benjamin felt very small and tired. He picked Grimalkin up for comfort, and stumbled across the road, his knapsack thumping against his back. "If only I did not have to see everyone in the inn!" he confided to Grimalkin. "They may laugh at my lumps of red and yellow earth or hold their noses at our smell of smoke and bear's grease."

Just then the door of the inn opened and Mamma slipped out into the courtyard.

"Mamma!" called Benjamin softly.

"Benjamin, have thee and Grimalkin returned?"

"Mamma! I have something to show thee. Please to follow me to the horse shed."

Benjamin was no longer tired. He took the poplar board out of his knapsack and held it close to the lanthorn.

Even by the feeble light Mamma could tell that the picture was warm with color.

"Why, wherever did thee get color?" she exclaimed.

"From the earth, Mamma."

"And the Indian Chief? Is it not our good friend Sassoonan?"

"It is!"

"I am glad thee found Sassoonan. I need not have worried."

Grimalkin rubbed against Mamma's skirts to attract her attention.

"Aye, little one, I thought about thee, too," she said.

A cool wind was rising. Mamma untied her apron and wrapped it about her shoulders.

"Benjamin," she said slowly, thoughtfully, "does thee know that color is not necessary to thy well-being?"

"Aye," piped Benjamin in a small voice.

"It is not like the sun that warms, or the rain that freshens, or the bread that nourishes. Does thee know that?"

"Yes, Mamma. I know."

"Very well then. I shall give thee a stick of my indigo blue. With red and yellow from the earth and with blue from my dye pot, thee can blend all the tints in the rainbow."

Benjamin turned his back to the light. He was suddenly afraid his happiness might spill over into tears.

Mamma must have had a talk with Papa, for after that night Benjamin was given a little corner of his own by the chimney place. There each evening he sat over his drawing board while Grimalkin curled himself at the very edge of the board where he watched through half-shut eyes.

The guests gathered about Benjamin in openmouthed wonder. "Forsooth!" they exclaimed. "Here is a lad who can paint anything from a portrait to a landscape. What is more," they remarked, "you can tell the one from the other! Ah, to be a boy again! Nary a care in the world."

But Benjamin *did* have a care, and it irritated him like a wood nettle in his shirt. What good were all the colors of the rainbow? What good were they if he could not lay them on smoothly?

He tried his forefinger, but it was too pudgy. The color spread where he did not want it to go. He tried duck feathers, but they made the color spatter. He whittled a tiny wooden paddle, but that did not seem to carry enough color. It dried off in the split second it took to move from the paint cup to the drawing board!

One night Benjamin decided to try a dry reed of timothy grass. He was doing, from memory, a portrait of Dr. Jonathan Moris at the time. The portrait was nearly done. Benjamin had only to color Dr. Moris' bright red wig. He was unmindful of the guests who stood behind his stool, watching.

Suddenly a great blob of red paint spilled from the reed and fell squarely on the tip of Dr. Moris' nose.

"Oh!" gasped Benjamin, and Grimalkin yowled nervously at the distress in his voice.

The onlookers broke out in loud laughter.

Benjamin whirled around in anger. He saw wagoners and a traveling tinker and scissors-grinder holding their sides. Their heads were thrown back, their mouths wide open, like cats on a fence. Only one among them did not laugh. It was Uncle Phineas Pennington from Philadelphia. He took out his pocket handkerchief and helped blot up the color.

"Uncle Phineas," said Benjamin through tight lips, "thee is a great merchant in the city of Philadelphia. Thee must know *real* painters. How do they apply their color?"

Uncle Phineas folded his pocket handkerchief.

"I am told," he said, "that they use hair pencils. In no wise have I seen them myself, mind thee," he hastened to add. "I have only heard tell of them."

"Hair pencils?"

"Aye, hair pencils."

"But what kind of hair, Uncle?"

"Camel's hair fastened in a goose quill."

Benjamin grew thoughtful. "Are there any camels in Penn's Province?"

"No," replied Uncle Phineas. "They live on a desert in Africa."

Sick at heart, Benjamin laid the portrait of Dr. Moris on the fire. He watched it burn to ashes and at last went upstairs.

Grimalkin padded softly behind him. When Benjamin was ready for bed, Grimalkin put out the candle with his paw and burrowed under the covers.

Benjamin's sleep was fitful. He crossed the desert in his dreams. He sat astride a huge camel that had a peculiar rocking gait, unlike any creature in Chester County. Even in his dreams he felt a kind of seasickness come over him.

At last the camel knelt on his cushioned knees so that Benjamin could dismount. Then he broke into rough laughter. "I've heard about such as you," he snorted. "You paint a man's portrait and then make a clown of him with a red nose. Fie on you!"

9. The Scratchings of Little Ben

THE next day Benjamin put his earth colors and his indigo blue away. Beside them he laid the duck feathers, the wooden paddle and the reed pen.

"I don't care a fig about color!" he pretended to Grimalkin that afternoon when chores were done.

It was a day late in November. Outside the wind howled and sent the inn signboard creaking on its hinges. All was cozy within the low-ceilinged kitchen. Mamma was at the loom, Hannah at the churn.

Grimalkin gazed up at Benjamin with searching eyes. Then he hooked his forepaw around Benjamin's wrist and drew him down so that the boy and the cat were looking eye to eye.

"What is it, kitling?" asked Benjamin. "Would thee like to sit for thy portrait? But mind thee, it will be in charcoal—black as thy fur."

Grimalkin gave an affectionate lick to Benjamin's hand. Then he whisked softly over to the hearth. There he put all four paws close together, sat down on his haunches, curved his tail closely about his feet, and smiled the way cats will.

"Never was there another cat so understanding!" laughed Benjamin. "Now if thee can just hold still, Grimalkin."

Grimalkin proved a fine sitter. He posed very quietly—except for the tipmost end of his tail, which moved up and down like a wee beckoning finger.

Benjamin worked rapidly. Soon the carts would come rumbling into the courtyard. Soon the inn would be alive with noisy travelers. Soon Grimalkin would grow weary of sitting and streak down cellar or upstairs.

He worked with quick, free strokes. He did not think of body, ears, eyes, legs, tail. He saw the whole cat at once.

There! The form was captured. Now he could strengthen the features to make this a portrait of a particular cat, Grimalkin.

He copied Grimalkin's eyes with their wonderfully long pupils. He drew the whiskers.

"Elmira's whiskers curve downward," he said as he worked. "Thy whiskers be different, Grimalkin. They bristle out straight and orderly, like the lines of my copybook."

Now Benjamin studied Grimalkin's tail. Its tip still twitched up and down, up and down.

Suddenly Benjamin caught his breath. "Why, that soft, silken tail!" he whispered.

His strokes became slower, slower; then stopped altogether. He swooped Grimalkin into his arms and raced up the stairs to his little cubbyhole of a room. He set Grimalkin on the floor, backed out the door, closed it firmly and fled down to the kitchen.

He began to collect articles from here, there and everywhere: Mamma's shears, a goose quill, Grimalkin's half-finished portrait. Then he rummaged in the bottom drawer of the pine dresser and found all of his jugs of paint and the stick of indigo.

Mamma at her loom and Hannah at the churn exchanged smiles.

"The scratchings of little Ben," said Hannah above the swishing noise of the churn.

Mamma nodded.

Back in his room, Benjamin carefully laid each article on his bench. As the pair of shears clattered against the paint jugs, Grimalkin whisked up the bedpost. Once as a kitten he had had his ear nipped by that very same pair of shears. One of the grownups had been cutting a cocklebur out of his fur and had accidentally pinched his ear.

"I recall the accident, too," said Benjamin comfortingly. "It shall not happen again. I promise thee."

Grimalkin leaped down onto the coverlet, and in that little instant Benjamin laid hold of him.

The fur on Grimalkin's back and tail bristled in fear.

"Why, how nice of thee to bristle up!" exclaimed Benjamin. "I can cut thy hair easily now."

And indeed he did. He cut the tapering hairs at the very tip of Grimalkin's tail.

"See! It didn't hurt thee a bit," murmured Benjamin as he tied the little bundle together with one of his own long hairs. Then he fixed it in the goose quill.

"How soft and silky!" he whispered as he brushed the hairs across his hand. "A camel's shaggy coat would not be near so fine."

Twilight was closing in. Benjamin moved his bench closer to the window. He poured some of the thick yellow earth paint into a mussel shell, added a few drops of indigo blue and stirred the mixture vigorously. Then he daubed a sample of the color on his hand and held it up to Grimalkin's eyes.

"It needs a mite more of the yellow," he said.

His heart beat fast. The color matched now. He brought the drawing board close to the light. With his new hair pencil he painted the eyes a clear green. The color did not spread. It did not spatter or spill. It went on so smoothly that not a single hair line showed.

The picture in Benjamin's hand trembled as he turned it around and faced it to the looking glass. Next he lifted Grimalkin and held the portrait and the cat side by side.

"Alike as a pair of boots!" he laughed. Then his face sobered. "Thee, Grimalkin, is my nighest friend," he said softly, earnestly. "When I am an old man with white curls, I shall remember how thee furnished my paintbrush."

And he pressed his head close against Grimalkin's.

10. Patchy as a Rag Bag

ALL that evening, in the chimney corner, Benjamin painted in a fever of excitement. He made a new portrait of Dr. Jonathan Moris, and never once did the red color land where it was not intended.

"The doctor's red bush wig looks so natural," declared Papa, "I can nigh smell the pomade on it."

When the portrait was done, Benjamin painted indigo birds, and yellow-billed cuckoos, and foxes and weasels.

The evening flew. By the time Grimalkin snuffed out the candle to remind everyone that it was bedtime, Benjamin had painted six pictures. With the sixth picture came a horrible discovery. The paintbrush was not going to last. In fact, it was worn out already!

In the days that followed, Grimalkin played a kind of hide-and-seek with Benjamin. Whenever he spied Benjamin coming toward him, shears in hand, he vanished like a puff of smoke. One time he flew up the scarecrow's breeches and hid for almost an hour.

But at last Grimalkin made a discovery. If he sat very still while Benjamin cut a tuft of hair from his coat, he was rewarded with the most delicious tidbits—a nubbin of roast pork or venison, a crumb of shoo-fly pie, some freshly cracked nut meats, a dollop of soft white cheese.

And quite as pleasant as the tidbits were Benjamin's words of praise. "Thee is beautiful. Thee is comely in spite of everything," Benjamin would murmur softly as he snipped the little tufts of fur. "What if thy coat be fleckered? The light in thy eyes is like a candle. Thee is a true Quaker. Sober, patched coat, but shining spirit within."

Grimalkin would roll over and over in happiness. Then he would chase his tail until Benjamin grew dizzy watching him.

Soon Grimalkin did not fear the shears at all. He was ready and willing to furnish all the paintbrushes his master could use. He seemed to know he was important and *needed*. He walked about, waving his shorn tail as gaily as if it had been a flag. And the patchier he grew, the closer he clung to Benjamin. Had not Benjamin saved his life? Now he, Grimalkin, was returning a favor!

"Mamma," questioned Papa one day, "has thee or the girls accidentally scalded our Grimalkin?"

"No, Papa," replied Mamma with concern in her voice. "I have asked the girls that very question."

Papa stooped down and stroked Grimalkin. "Is thee ailing, little one?"

"The mange, likely," said Mamma, "or some winter illness

that will vanish with the snow's melting." But Mamma's words sounded more hopeful than her voice.

"Patchy as a rag bag!" sighed Papa. "He minds me of a piebald horse I had as a boy." And he shook his head sadly.

No one suspected the real cause of Grimalkin's appearance. Yet each one of the family tried to remedy it.

Mamma saved all the giblets from chickens, geese and wild turkeys for Grimalkin. What did it matter if the gravy had no savor? Better to restore Grimalkin's health, she thought.

Papa, who was very fond of kidney pie, gave all the kidneys on his plate to Grimalkin.

The girls, too, tried to coax Grimalkin's appetite. They saved little dabs of whipped sillabub and floating island pudding for him. They even saved the knucklebones and ham marrow that usually went to Papa's hound dogs.

As for the boys, they slyly offered little morsels to Grimalkin underneath the table board: squash and succotash, mussels and shad.

Every day was feast day for Grimalkin. He scarcely had time to lick the flavor left on his lips. Always there seemed to be a new and more tempting morsel set before him.

Meanwhile, Benjamin went his way, unmindful of all the worry he had caused. He went to school. He did his chores. He painted his pictures.

"No need to tell our little wren," Mamma had whispered to each of the family in turn. "He will learn of Grimalkin's ailment soon enough."

Grimalkin, however, grew plump as a pig being fattened for market. But his fur did not improve. It became steadily worse.

One First Day evening on the edge of winter Papa led the way into the parlor for the quiet hour of family worship.

A lone candle made black shadows on the wall. The fire in the hearth burned softly as if it, too, were at worship.

The family settled itself on small benches, Mamma and the girls on one side of the parlor, the boys on the other. Behind Benjamin sat Thomas and John, their knees at his back. On either side were Joseph and Samuel. Papa sat facing everyone.

With effort Benjamin folded his hands across his chest the way the elders and the overseers did. Then he sat in cramped silence, waiting for God to put words into Papa's mouth.

Suddenly there was a light patter of cushioned feet, and Grimalkin was in the room. He sat down before Papa and busied himself, washing his paws and dressing what little fur he had left.

Papa's voice began to quake. "Winter closes in, O Lord," he said. "Thou hast provided well for Thy human creatures. Now we beseech Thee to restore Grimalkin's coat to its former thickness."

Papa's voice died away. The room became very still. Benjamin found it difficult to breathe. Even the candle sputtered for air.

I must tell Papa. Now. At once, Benjamin told himself. He leaned forward. His heart seemed to catch in his throat. He opened his mouth, but no sound escaped. Then, all of a sudden, the words tumbled out like water over a mill wheel.

"Papa! Grimalkin is not ailing. I have been making hair pencils from his coat. Uncle Phineas told me that real painters use hair pencils made from camel's hair. But camels live far away on a desert. I had to use Grimalkin's hair instead."

Benjamin stopped for breath. Joseph and Samuel seemed to be closing in on him. Thomas' and John's knees were boring into his back.

After a long while he dared to look up.

Papa's face was like a sky that promises thunder and suddenly clears. His brow clouded. Then all at once he broke into a slow smile.

" 'Necessity can sharpen the wits even of children,' " he said. "To make use of the gifts at hand is workmanlike. From now on, however, thee will leave Grimalkin's coat untouched."

Benjamin's mouth opened in amazement. Papa, he concluded, was a wonderful man.

11. A Box from Philadelphia

By SPRING Benjamin noticed that Grimalkin's fur was coming in thick and sleek again.

I can bear to give up painting with color to save Grimalkin's fur, he thought to himself one April afternoon when he was driving the cows home. Though spring paints a high green, he sighed, and I long to do the same.

Grimalkin frisked on ahead. Every now and then he stopped to jump straight up in the air for no reason at all—unless he, too, knew that it was spring.

Benjamin had tied a bell around Grimalkin's neck to warn the birds. His tiny bell tinkled now above the deeper tones made by the clappers in the cowbells. Together they played a kind of peaceful tune.

Benjamin was so busy with his thoughts that he did not hear a journeyman approaching. He looked up suddenly, and there the stranger was, reining in his horse, waiting for Benjamin to lead the cattle across the narrow, rutted road.

The stranger cupped his hand to his mouth.

"Could this be Benjamin West and Grimalkin?" he called out.

"Why, yes!" replied Benjamin, his eyes round with wonder. "How's thee know?"

The man laughed. "Your Uncle Phineas Pennington paints a good portrait—with words," he said. "I've just stopped at Door-Latch Inn. Left a present there for a lad of the name of Benjamin West and a small remembrance for a cat of the name of Grimalkin."

Usually Benjamin liked to linger in the steamy warmth of the barn. But tonight he had no time. Those presents from the city. What could they be? Some wondrous surprise from the warehouses on the water front? From England? From Spain? From Africa?

He lifted Grimalkin to his shoulder and raced for the inn. "Presents for us?" he asked breathlessly as he burst into the kitchen.

"Aye!" cried Sarah and Hannah and Mary and Elizabeth in chorus. Then they all began talking at once.

"It rattles like trinkets."

"No, it's too heavy for trinkets."

"Uncle Phineas sent it."

"Uncle Phineas favors thee and Grimalkin."

"I'll help thee open it."

"No. I'll help."

"Peace!" called Mamma above the din. "Here, son. Set the box carefully on the table board. Now, then, we can *all* watch thee open it."

There was a sudden flurry and Grimalkin had leaped up on the table, full of curiosity.

Benjamin lifted the package with trembling hands. He undid the stout hemp cord. He laid back the folds of paper. He lifted the lid. And there, looking out at him, was a *real* picture. A picture that he himself had not painted!

There were trees in the picture, so lifelike their leaves seemed to stir. There was a waterfall, too, so white and churning that it seemed to Benjamin he could feel the spray on his face.

He took the picture out of its box and read the name in the corner. "Grevling," he said.

"Look!" cried Mary. "There's another picture."

"And another, and another, and still another," said Mamma quietly.

A moment ago Benjamin had never seen a real picture. Now he held six of them. For his very own.

"Oh! Oh!" cried Mary again. "Underneath the pictures are some canvas and two boxes! Here, let *me* hold the pictures. See what's in the boxes."

Benjamin handed the pictures and the pieces of canvas to Mary. He lifted the cover of the smaller box very cautiously, and then burst into laughter.

"What is it? What is it?" shrieked the girls.

"A bunch of catmint for Grimalkin."

"But the other box! Open it quickly."

Benjamin stood very still. The blood throbbed in his head.

"It's a paintbox," he said in awe. He lifted it out and ran his fingers over the shiny black tin box, the little oblong bricks of color, all in a row, the tiny glass bottle for water, and last of all the hair pencils. There were fat ones and thin ones, and middle-sized ones.

Grimalkin had to see, too. He left his catmint and came over to pat the colors very gently as if they were petals of a flower. He smelled of the brushes.

"Ho!" laughed Benjamin. "These do not feel like brushes made from a cat's fur. They must be camel's hair. Why, they are! They are! It says so!"

Benjamin was too excited for sleep that night. Every time he drowsed off, he would waken with a jolt. Then his fingers would reach out from under the quilt to treasure the little tin paintbox on the bench beside his bed.

"It's true!" he would whisper to Grimalkin who lay curled at his back. Then, satisfied that all was well, both the boy and the cat would doze off again.

The next morning after breakfast Benjamin appeared to be setting off for school.

But when he had gone around the house, he entered the front door, raced up the stairway used by the guests, gathered his presents from Uncle Phineas, and climbed up the ladderlike steps to the garret.

Grimalkin whisked ahead of him, an inky shadow in the gloom of the garret.

Quietly Benjamin closed the trap door. Then he opened the windows in the gable ends, and threw wide the shutters.

Sunlight came dancing in. It touched off the strings of herbs swinging from the rafters. It picked out the letters that said *Welcome* on the old wooden sea chest.

Benjamin laughed. "How nice of thee, Grandpa Pearson, to bid me welcome to use thy sea chest!"

He opened the lid, resting it against the low, slanting roof. Then he stood the pictures from Uncle Phineas inside the lid.

"I wish *I* had done these!" he sighed, studying first one and then another.

He opened the little tin paintbox, and in a moment was lost in the adventure of creating a picture.

He forgot about school as if it had never been. He was growing trees and building waterfalls—with a paintbrush!

Grimalkin, too, was busy with his own affairs. There was an

old round knapsack standing in a dark corner of the garret. It was made of some woolly stuff, and it had eyelets around the top through which straps were laced.

Little gray mice had discovered two empty eyelets just large enough to admit a mouse. Grimalkin spent hours watching for tiny sharp-nosed faces to peek out of the eyelets.

When Benjamin's fingers grew cold, he would box with Grimalkin. Or he would swing on the wooden pins that held the rafters in place.

The hours flew. Often he caught himself humming like a tea-kettle. Happiness seemed to bubble up inside him whenever he painted.

For three whole days—except for mealtimes—Benjamin and Grimalkin lived in the garret. They were never late for meals. Grimalkin's appetite was more dependable than a sundial. Promptly at mealtime he would cuff Benjamin on the ankle and give him no peace until he laid down his brush.

And just as Mamma was dipping up the gravy or ladling porridge into bowls, Benjamin and Grimalkin would be there.

On the afternoon of the third day, Benjamin was startled to hear the blasting voice of Master Snevely.

"Thy son!" the voice trumpeted. "Is he ailing?"

Benjamin strained his ears, but could hear no answer.

"For three days," the voice boomed upward, "his seat has been vacant."

Again the house was muffled in stillness.

Benjamin held his breath. At last the *rat-a-tat* of hoofbeats growing fainter and fainter drifted up to him.

With a sigh of relief he went on painting the foliage of a hickory tree

Suddenly there were light footsteps on the ladder. Then the trap door creaked open. A starched white cap showed above the opening, then a pair of troubled blue eyes.

"Mamma!" gasped Benjamin. "What have I done? I have not even thought about school."

Mamma's lips thinned into a firm line as she mounted the last few steps and walked the length of the garret. Her eyes seemed to throw off sparks.

"Benjamin!" she said sharply. "It pains me . . ." And then she stopped short as she caught sight of the picture. Benjamin had not copied Grevling. But he had learned some of his secrets.

He had learned how to make water ripple in the wind and how to make the sun touch off the underside of leaves.

"Put down thy brush," she said softly. "Another stroke might spoil it."

12. Make a Merchant of Him

"BENJAMIN WEST!" commanded Schoolmaster Snevely the following morning. "Stand before thy schoolfellows."

It was only a few steps to Master Snevely's desk, but to Benjamin it seemed hours away. His legs felt stiff and old.

"Make haste! Now then. Face about."

The room grew silent.

"For three days," the schoolmaster said as he shook three bony fingers in Benjamin's face, "for three days thy schoolfellows mourned thee as dreadful ill. Instead, hidden in the garret, thee painted with bold, gaudy colors."

Benjamin could feel his schoolfellows' eyes on him. They seemed to be boring little holes through him. The only comforting sound was made by Grimalkin scratching in the wood box outside the door.

"For punishment thee will remain after school, cutting and mending the goose-quill pens."

"Aye, sir. I shall stay this very night."

Master Snevely's eyes narrowed. *"This* night," he replied with a sniff, "and every night until the last quarter of the year."

"Why, that is five months!" said Benjamin half aloud.

"It is, indeed. And a light punishment for wasting time on needless things."

Spring and summer passed. By the time autumn came in, the very sight of a goose sickened Benjamin. All he could think of was, Here is the creature who provides my punishment. He was glad when early one morning Grimalkin hissed right back at a gander and flew at him until the courtyard was a blizzard of feathers.

That same evening as Benjamin worked over his pens the school-master broke his rule of silence.

"Lad," he asked, "how does thee feel about geese by now? Speak truly."

Benjamin looked up in surprise. "Grimalkin and I are of one mind about them," he said quickly. "We can't abide their hissing and honking."

Master Snevely made a noise in his throat that strangely resembled a chuckle. "My feeling is the same," he announced. "I have been eating nothing but goose and gander for the past fortnight. A bolt of lightning struck the flock owned by my landlady. Since then I breakfast on goose. I dine on goose. I sup on goose. Sometimes the goose is masked in gravy. Sometimes it peers out from underneath turnips. Sometimes it lurks in a pudding-pie. But *always* it is there!"

Then the schoolmaster's eyes lighted with an idea. "I have a

mind," he said, "to sup at Door-Latch Inn tonight. The talk of journeymen and the smell of good cooking may whet my appetite."

If Mamma and the girls had overheard Master Snevely, they could not have prepared a tastier supper.

There was bean porridge with thick chunks of salt pork. There were hot brown bread with fresh butter, and pod peas. And for dessert Mamma had made apple fancy and hot chocolate, a rare treat even for Door-Latch Inn.

Thirty, in all, sat down to eat. And to Benjamin's delight, Uncle Phineas was among them, making everyone feel at ease.

Even Master Snevely tapped his foot with pleasure when Uncle Phineas chanted:

> "I eat my peas with honey,
> I've done it all my life.
> It makes the peas taste funny,
> But it keeps them on my knife."

Finally Uncle Phineas loosened his leather girdle and turned to Papa.

"What would thee say to my taking Benjamin to Philadelphia for a fortnight?"

Benjamin held his breath until his chest hurt. His eyes darted like arrows from Papa's face to Mamma's, then to Master Snevely's. He was unmindful of everyone else in the room.

Papa stroked his beard, thinking of all the reasons why Benjamin should not go. "School. Chores," he said. "Chores. School."

"What does *thee* think?" he asked of the schoolmaster.

Benjamin shuddered.

"The boy," said Master Snevely, shaking his head gravely, "is not so quick in his sums as I would have him, but of late he has been diligent. He has cut enough goose-quill pens to last out my days as a master. A journey may teach him the importance of sums. I am favorable to the plan."

Benjamin's eyes opened wide in astonishment.

"Mamma?" questioned Papa.

"I want to say 'yes,' " said Mamma, smoothing her apron. "And I want to say 'no.' A whole day's journey from home is a long way for our little wren."

Papa flinched. Pet names annoyed him. Little wren indeed! He turned to Uncle Phineas.

"Mamma is right," he said. "The answer is 'yes.' Take him along, Phineas. He may forget his notions about painting. Make a merchant of him. Aye, make a merchant of him."

Suddenly Benjamin's happiness faded. What of Grimalkin? A trip without Grimalkin would be only half a trip.

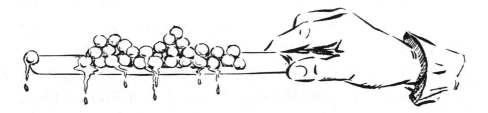

13. An Old Black Coat

"PAPA," Benjamin questioned as they stood side by side at the wash bench next morning, "could I take——"

"As touching Grimalkin," Papa interrupted, "do not worry. I will caution Mamma and the girls to see to his happiness."

Breakfast had no flavor that morning. No matter how much milk Benjamin poured over his porridge, it seemed to lodge in his throat. He was glad when the meal was over and he could slip out of doors. He watched the travelers load their wagons and set off together in a long pack train. As they turned out of the yard, Benjamin ran alongside the driver. "Should thee someday see a lad of the name of Jacob Ditzler . . ." he said breathlessly and then stopped in embarrassment.

The driver slowed down.

"And what if we do?" he said, not unkindly.

"Please . . . please to tell him that Grimalkin is well and I am going to Philadelphia this day."

The man nodded gravely, and the women and children stared after Benjamin, making him feel quite important.

He strode back toward the courtyard where Uncle Phineas was strapping their knapsacks to his big pacer's saddle, while all of the family looked on.

Benjamin felt a gentle hand on his shoulder. It was Mamma holding out an old black coat that once had belonged to brother Samuel.

"The north wind blows raw and sharp for autumn," she said anxiously. "Samuel's coat worn over thy own coat will help to keep thee warm."

Benjamin frowned. He did not want to go to Philadelphia wearing two coats! And just when he was about to explain how warm he was, he swallowed his words. He looked at Samuel's coat as if he had never really seen it before. His eyes brightened. How big and roomy is Samuel's coat! he said to himself. Why, it would hold . . . a cat . . . extremely well.

He took the coat with a polite thank-you, then ran toward the inn, slipping his arms into the sleeves as he ran. "I just now remembered something in my room," he explained.

He looked back over his shoulder and smiled to see Grimalkin bounding after him.

A few moments later he stood breathless at the upping block.

"I declare!" exclaimed Papa. "Thee looks as stuffed as a pudding bag in Samuel's coat."

Benjamin laughed nervously. Grimalkin was a strong, active cat. He was not used to being buttoned inside a coat, and every time he squirmed he either tickled Benjamin's ribs or sent his

claws into Benjamin's flesh. To cover the wriggling motions about his waist, Benjamin folded his arms and scratched himself lightly, trying his best to quiet Grimalkin.

"Phineas," said Papa, "Mamma and I have made out a list of things we are needing."

Benjamin suddenly looked down in horror. Grimalkin's pink nose peeked out of a buttonhole which he had left open as a porthole.

He glanced around quickly to see if anyone had noticed, but everyone was listening to Papa.

Why was it, Benjamin asked himself, that home always looked so good just when he was about to leave it! He had felt the very same way on his first day of school, and on the first day he rode to Miller Clinkenbeard's.

Mamma mistook Benjamin's searching glance for quite another reason.

"I must confess—" she shook her head—"it seems strange that Grimalkin is not here to say good-by to thee. It is not like him."

Papa stood thoughtful a moment. "A gopher, likely," he mused. "Grimalkin ever was fond of an early morning hunt."

At sound of his name Grimalkin tried to squeeze out of the little porthole.

Quick as a flash Benjamin clapped his hand over his stomach.

"Is thee ailing, little wren?" asked Mamma.

"No, Mamma!" replied Benjamin, his face reddening. "I am fine!"

"He appears feverish to me," said Sarah. "And from the way he is scratching he may be breaking out with the measles."

"The prospect of adventure always brings blood to the traveler's face," replied Uncle Phineas as he mounted and gave a hand to Benjamin. "Is thee comfortable perched behind me?"

"Oh, yes!" exclaimed Benjamin in a panic, for Grimalkin was now exploring the back of Samuel's coat and mewing faintly.

"Let us be off," he begged in a voice loud enough to drown out Grimalkin's cries.

Uncle Phineas' horse pawed the ground in agreement.

"Easy there," cried Uncle Phineas, and the big pacer swung out of the courtyard while the family shouted words that Benjamin could not hear.

Benjamin's right hand and forearm were fastened securely about Uncle Phineas' belt. With his left hand he now unbuttoned four more buttons of Samuel's coat. He could feel Grimalkin scrabbling around for an exit. He could see Grimalkin's head peer out like an opossum from its mother's pouch.

Benjamin heaved a great sigh of relief. They were safely off at last! Now they could both enjoy the sights and the smells of autumn.

"Stroke Grimalkin for me," chuckled Uncle Phineas.

"How's thee know?" gasped Benjamin.

"Because," laughed Uncle Phineas, "I saw a black tail wave from between the flaps of thy coat as I helped thee mount. I knew thee could not possibly have sprouted a tail so quickly."

14. The City of Brotherly Love

How could a boy be homesick with a traveling companion like Uncle Phineas? As they jogged along, he told such wondrous tales of Philadelphia that Benjamin's imagination flew on ahead.

They passed farm carts loaded with wheat and cabbages and pigs and chickens and flax and corn for the market in Philadelphia. But Benjamin hardly saw them.

In his mind's eye he was already there! He pretended he was a big, pompous man followed by a black cat and a slave pushing a wheelbarrow. He was striding from market stall to market stall, tasting little samples of butter and cheese, then stopping to let the black cat lick his fingers. When his half-boots came untied, the slave had to kneel down and tie them. No matter what went wrong, the slave had to fix it. At last he bought some huge turtles and lobsters, a firkin of butter and cheese, a suckling pig, a gammon of bacon, a skipple of salt, and led the way home, his nose in the air.

To the pleasant music of Uncle Phineas' voice and the steady hoofbeats of the big sorrel, Benjamin went on with his make-believe. He pretended next that he was the slave, pushing the wheelbarrow along the rough block pavement of the market street. On every hand he was bumped and jostled. He could feel his back and arms ache with the weight of the load. He could feel the perspiration run down his face. In fact, with Uncle Phineas acting as a windbreak and with Grimalkin's furry warmth and Samuel's extra coat, and the sun climbing higher and higher, Benjamin actually was perspiring!

He tapped Uncle Phineas on the shoulder. "Uncle!"

"Yes?"

"I am glad I am a Quaker like Papa. He says it is wrong to have slaves."

"So it is!" replied Uncle Phineas as he brushed a low-hanging branch out of his way. "And especially in a city like Philadelphia. Does thee know what the name Philadelphia means?"

"No, Uncle."

"Philadelphia is a Greek word. It means brotherly love."

"How did the Indians happen to choose a Greek name?" asked Benjamin, puzzled.

Uncle Phineas slapped his thigh. "They didn't," he laughed. "They called it *Coaquannock,* which means a grove of tall pines."

"Are the pines still there?"

"Not all of them, to be sure. Some are ships' masts now. They sail the seas, then come back to rest in the port of Philadelphia, in sight of the very hills where they grew."

"Uncle Phineas, thee would have made a fine schoolmaster!" sighed Benjamin as he lifted Grimalkin to his shoulder.

They were traveling over low roads now and early fall rains had churned them up. "Used to be we spoke of *spring* as mudtime," mused Uncle Phineas. "Now it appears we have mudtime in autumn, too."

He fell silent, watching to see that his horse did not step in a chuckhole. The only sound to be heard was the sucking noise made by the sorrel's hoofs and Grimalkin's rumbly purring.

The town crier was calling the hour of seven when Uncle Phineas and Benjamin and Grimalkin arrived in the City of Brotherly Love. Lanthorns twinkled in the entryways of the big brick houses. Slits of candlelight escaped through the shutters.

Uncle Phineas was a bachelor and lived at the Penny Pot Inn. As they walked into the great room of the inn, a joint of meat was turning on a spit before the fire. Instead of a boy turning the roast, it was managed by a little dog running in a treadmill cage.

Grimalkin high-tailed it for the hearth. He licked up all the little spatters of gravy, then sat hopefully waiting for more. "Turn faster! Faster!" he seemed to say. "I'm well-nigh starved."

Benjamin was tired, and the poor turnspit dog looked so tired, too, that a great wave of homesickness came over him. Perhaps it was not homesickness alone. Added to it was the hot feeling of guilt for sneaking Grimalkin away.

Suddenly he was asking the innkeeper for a piece of paper and laboriously trying to write with a goose-quill pen that needed mending. Slowly the letters took form.

For
John West
To be left at Door-Latch Inn
near Springfield
in Chester County

Philadelphia,

the 28th of the $\dfrac{10}{mo}$ 1746

Dear Papa and Mamma—Grimalkin is with me. He traveled well in Samuel's coat. I am sorry for hiding him. It was dreadful wrong of me. I hope to mend my ways, and hope thee will not mind paying the fourpence postage.

Thy loveing son·

Benjn

Luckily a postrider happened to be leaving for the west. He added Benjamin's letter to the others in his saddlebag and thundered off into the night.

Benjamin watched him out of sight. Then he trudged back to the hearth.

"A good hot meal is what thee needs," smiled Uncle Phineas.

And it was indeed! Benjamin ate a great slice of beef, although he had not meant to at all because of the poor turnspit dog. He finally made a bargain with himself. He would ask for a second slice and save half of it for the dog and half for Grimalkin. Then he felt better at once.

When the innkeeper's daughter set a porringer of peas on the table with a little jug of honey, both Benjamin and Uncle Phineas recited together:

> "I eat my peas with honey,
> I've done it all my life.
> It makes the peas taste funny,
> But it keeps them on my knife."

All homesickness was gone.

15. On the Banks of the Delaware

PHILADELPHIA is a world in itself," Uncle Phineas told Benjamin the next morning. "And it is thine and Grimalkin's to explore. Listen sharp, lad. My shop is on Winn Street. Penny Pot Inn is hard by the River Delaware. The market is on High Street. Commit that to memory and thee will never get lost."

Neither the cat nor the boy got beyond the River Delaware. In the whole County of Chester, Grimalkin had never seen rats so monstrous and lively. As for Benjamin, his eyes flew over the harbor. Now he knew why Jacob Ditzler wanted to come back to Philadelphia when he was man-grown. *Here* were things to see! Ships building. River boats and ships of the sea. Single-masted sloops. Two-masted brigs. Ships that carried a hundred ton!

As they made their way down to the water front Benjamin spied a string of rawhide lying discarded in front of a warehouse. Suddenly he had an idea. He picked up the string and quickly made it into a cat's collar with a long lead. Now he could explore the wharves without fear of losing Grimalkin.

Together they visited all of the sail lofts. They saw apprentice boys sitting on low stools, mending sails with great long needles. They saw boys twisting hemp into ships' ropes. Without stopping their work, the boys eyed Grimalkin curiously. Benjamin studied every face. Somewhere among the young apprentices he hoped to find the eager round face of Jacob Ditzler. But not one among the boys even resembled him. Perhaps, thought Benjamin, he is among the sailors loading or unloading the ships. Together the boy and the cat trudged the full length of the wharf, but most of the sailors they saw were grown men. Benjamin inquired at every warehouse, too, but no one had heard of a boy named Jacob Ditzler.

By midday Benjamin was tired and discouraged. He shared a piece of journeycake with Grimalkin. Then they both curled up in the shelter of a long wooden shed and dozed in the sun.

Just as they were falling into a deep sleep, they woke with a start. Steeple bells were clanging. Guns were saluting. And from all the red houses up and down the hillsides people came running.

"What is it?" asked Benjamin of a lad who almost stumbled over Benjamin's feet.

The boy was running so fast he could not stop. "The *Antelope Packet*," he called over his shoulder. "She's almost ready to dock."

Benjamin scooped Grimalkin into his arms and raced in the direction of Winn Street.

"Uncle! Uncle!" he cried as he burst into Uncle Phineas' shop. "The city has come alive. I need a paintbox!"

A slow smile spread over Uncle Phineas' face. He reached far back on a shelf and produced a clean canvas and a paintbox exactly like the one he had sent Benjamin.

The bells were still clanging. The guns were still saluting as Benjamin set up his canvas on the banks of the Delaware. Grimalkin patted and sniffed the cakes of paint. Then he settled down at Benjamin's feet and blinked up as if to say, "This seems almost like home. Now I can take a real snooze."

Sailors from Spain and Portugal, from New England and old England, from the West Indies and the Azores gathered about Benjamin. Few spoke the same language. But they all understood the picture that took shape before their eyes. A shining river going out to sea. Men fishing on the banks. A ship in the harbor. And a white cow eying the water.

Perhaps Benjamin would not have painted so easily had he seen the scarlet chariot of Samuel Shoemaker draw up behind him.

Samuel Shoemaker was known throughout the colonies as a big merchant. If Uncle Phineas had five boxes of salt in his warehouse, Samuel Shoemaker had twenty and five. If Uncle Phineas had ten rolls, each, of calico and cambric, Samuel Shoemaker had ten times ten, and silks and velvets besides.

After handing the reins to a slave, Samuel Shoemaker threaded his way through the crowd of sailors and tapped Benjamin on the shoulder with his gold-headed cane.

Benjamin looked around in surprise. He had never seen a man quite like this before. His face was as plain as a salt box, but his wig and his clothes were wonderful to behold. His wig was tied to resemble pigeons' wings at the sides. And he wore a purple waistcoat with a cascade of white ruffles that reminded Benjamin of the waterfall in Grevling's picture.

"Lad, who are you?" asked Samuel Shoemaker, his eyes on the canvas rather than on Benjamin.

"Why, I am Benjamin West, son of John West," replied Benjamin in a voice so like Papa's that Benjamin scarcely knew it for his own. "I come from Door-Latch Inn, in the Township of Springfield, in the County of Chester."

The man threw back his head and laughed so vigorously that the powder from his wig rose like a white fog. "Egad!" he whistled. "You must be Pennington's nephew. I am Samuel Shoemaker."

"Thee knows my Uncle Phineas?" asked Benjamin.

"La, yes! Here is the proof."

And right there on the banks of the Delaware with all the sailors tapping their feet to the tune, the great Samuel Shoemaker recited:

> "I eat my peas with honey,
> I've done it all my life.
> It makes the peas taste funny,
> But it keeps them on my knife."

When the foot-tapping and the laughter died away, Mr. Shoemaker said: "I have just ordered a picture from the artist William Williams. I am on my way to his lodgings now and should be glad of your company."

"But I—I have a cat——"

Mr. Shoemaker looked down at Grimalkin, who was now sniffing his shoe buckles.

"A mannerly cat is welcome anywhere," he nodded.

"Why, that is what Mamma says. Her very words!" smiled Benjamin as he handed Mr. Shoemaker his paintbox.

Carrying his picture very carefully in one arm and Grimalkin in the other, Benjamin climbed into the chariot while the sailors thumped one another on the back and grinned at his good fortune.

William Williams was a little cricket of a man who had gone to sea in his youth. He lived in a small studio with hardly any furniture. But to Benjamin it was the most beautiful room he had ever seen. Canvases lined the walls. And from them pink flamingo birds and ships' captains and parrots and white-wigged ladies and gentlemen looked down with a superior air. It was almost as if they could smell the turnips and cabbages cooking in the rooms below. To Benjamin, however, no room had ever smelled more exciting. He sifted out the familiar cooking odors and breathed in the good smell of paints and oils.

Mr. Shoemaker seemed in a hurry to leave. He introduced Benjamin and Grimalkin, asked when his picture would be delivered, then turned to go. "I'll leave you two artists alone," he said with a wink. "You'll have much to talk about."

But when the door was closed Benjamin seemed to be struck dumb. He wanted to ask a million questions. Yet he could think of none.

At last William Williams thought of a question. "What books," said he, "have you read?"

"Why, I've read the Bible. I've read about John and Thomas and Samuel and Joseph. My brothers were named for them."

"I mean books on the art of painting," said Mr. Williams with a slow smile.

"Oh," gulped Benjamin in surprise. "Are there books on painting?"

For answer Mr. Williams reached up on his chimney shelf and took down two sizable volumes. They were bound in brown leather that had the nice look of an old saddle.

There was a kind of worship in the way Mr. Williams held them. "These two authors are Richardson and Dufresnoy. They were my teachers," he said as he looked down at Benjamin. "Now they can be yours, too." And he laid the books in Benjamin's hands.

Just then Grimalkin began to mew hungrily.

"Yo-ho!" laughed Mr. Williams. "Here is a cat that wants his dinner. Now it so happens that a lady who is sitting for her portrait just brought me a whortleberry pie and a crock of fresh milk. I'll heat the pie to make it juicy and toothsome. Meanwhile we can speak about your picture."

Benjamin had eaten nothing but dry journeycake since breakfast. His mouth watered at the thought of hot whortleberry pie, but no sooner had Mr. Williams left the room than his appetite was gone. He wished he could hide the picture. A hundred doubts began pricking at his mind. Were the colors too bright? Did the cow stand out too sharply?

He had about decided to snatch up his picture and his cat and run down the flight of stairs when Mr. Williams returned with the pie and a basin of milk for Grimalkin. All the while that he set the milk on the floor and placed the pie in the warming oven at the side of the chimney, he had one eye on Benjamin's picture.

Benjamin stole a sly glance at his face. It was as blank as a wig rest. He listened for some word of criticism. None came. Instead, Mr. Williams reached for the tongs hanging at the side of the mantel, took a live ember from the fire, then slowly lighted his pipe.

And just when Benjamin could bear the silence no longer Mr. Williams spoke. Even then Benjamin could not tell how he felt, for all he said was, "Will you leave your picture with me, lad? I want to show it to Dr. Smith of the Academy."

16. "We Wish to Buy Them"

"CAN'T see that thee has changed much," said Papa when Benjamin and Grimalkin returned from Philadelphia.

"Except," said Papa, stroking his beard thoughtfully, "thee and Grimalkin be thinner while thy knapsack appears heavier."

"Yes, Papa. It is filled with presents—a parcel of thread for Mary, bone buttons for Sarah, a comb for Hannah and buckles for Elizabeth."

"Mere trifles," snorted Papa. "What gives it the bulk?"

"A johnnycake pan for Mamma, and . . ."

"And what?"

"Two books," replied Benjamin as he placed them in Papa's hand. "For thee—and me," he added in a weak voice.

Papa looked over the books, trying to make out their titles.

"My spectacles are on the candle shelf," he said. "Take the books inside. They will bear looking into."

That night Benjamin went to sleep to the pleasantest of sounds. Overhead, the small patter of rain on the cedar shingles. Below, Papa's voice reading aloud from Richardson's book on the art of painting. Benjamin strained his ears. He could not make out the words, but the tune was good. For when Papa's voice began to rise and fall and boom and quake, he was mightily pleased. Even Grimalkin could tell that. He burrowed deep in under the quilts and purred in his loud rumbly fashion, as he always did when Papa and The Family were at peace.

As the news of Benjamin's trip spread, neighbors made all manner of excuses to visit Door-Latch Inn. They wanted to hear about the great Samuel Shoemaker. Mrs. Tomkins came down from the hills to borrow some live coals. The fire on her hearth had gone out, she said. However, she seemed in no hurry to get back home with her pot of glowing embers. She sat down on the settle while her eyes scoured the inn for a glimpse of Benjamin.

A spry-legged old man came ten miles to borrow duck eggs. "The creek on my place overflowed," he said. "Washed all my duck eggs downstream. Come to borry a few of yours, and maybe sit down a spell."

Only Mr. Wayne, a gentleman of Springfield, made no excuses. He dropped in one evening, purposely to watch Benjamin at work.

"By my life!" he exclaimed to Papa. "Your son's pictures are very acceptable. I should like to have one or two on my own mantel shelf. Then, when winter closes in, I could regard green trees and flowers. It would be like special windows opening onto spring."

Benjamin's heart sang. Never before had anyone *wanted* his pictures. Quickly he slipped down from his stool and opened the pine dresser. He selected three landscapes and three portraits, including his very favorite—that of Grimalkin.

"If it please thee, I should like to give these to Mr. Wayne," he said, handing the pictures to Papa.

Papa nodded. He seemed glad to get them out of the house.

The next morning when Benjamin was on his way to school, Mr. Wayne, on his black stallion, galloped up beside him. He leaped to the ground and led his horse along the road.

"My wife prizes the pictures," he smiled, as he fell into step with Benjamin. "Especially that of Grimalkin. She is overfond of cats, you know. 'Vastly pretty!' she exclaims every time she chances to look at it. I myself half expect the creature to miaow—he looks so lifelike. Mind my words, Benjamin, we shall soon be sending sitters to you for their portraits."

All this while Mr. Wayne had been jingling some coins in his pocket. Now he pulled out a whole handful of them and began counting. "One—two—three—four—five—six. Six dollars," he said, as he piled the money into a neat little stack. Then he

reached for Benjamin's hand and placed the money inside it.

"Mrs. Wayne and I wish to buy the pictures," he said. "And we hope a dollar apiece will please you."

"A dollar apiece!" repeated Benjamin. "Oh, Mr. Wayne . . . !" Then his throat filled and he could say no more.

All day long the words sang themselves over in Benjamin's heart. "Vastly pretty." "We wish to buy the pictures." "Vastly pretty." "We wish to buy the pictures." And in his pocket the six dollars kept a jingly tune to the words.

17. Pictures to Set Words on Fire

Now that Benjamin and Grimalkin were back home, it was almost as if they had never been gone.

Winter was closing in, and Benjamin had to take his place with Papa and his brothers. He dug turnips, piled them in a neat mound, and covered them with warm straw and earth. He husked corn. He gathered cattails for bed stuffing. He stacked swamp grass for the cows and bullocks. He helped yard the cattle.

Grimalkin was quite as busy as the rest of the family. Field mice were trying to find winter quarters at Door-Latch Inn, and there were days on end when he had to catch his sleep with one eye open.

The days wore into weeks. Weeks wore into months. But no word came from William Williams, or from Uncle Phineas either.

"Does thee suppose we dreamed that trip to Philadelphia?" whispered Benjamin to Grimalkin one long winter evening.

At that precise moment the door opened and in came a horseman. He pulled a letter from his boot and flourished it over his head. "For John West, Innkeeper," he announced as his eyes, unaccustomed to the firelight, tried to single out Mr. West.

Papa rose stiffly. He accepted the letter without even glancing at it. But Benjamin could see his hands tremble as he slipped it into his pocket.

"Thomas," he said, "see to the gentleman's horse.

"Hannah, be so good as to brew a cup of tea.

"Thee, Benjamin, carry warm water and fresh linen up to the front bedchamber."

Papa was first of all an innkeeper. Not until he had made certain that the rider and his horse were comfortable did he take the letter out of his pocket. Then he lighted a candle, clamped the candlestick over the back of his chair, put on his spectacles, and unfolded the fine white paper.

His fingers began drumming on the table board. The drumming grew louder as he read, louder even than the household noises: Mamma at her spinning wheel, the girls making *click-clack* noises with their knitting needles, Benjamin and the boys whittling treenails, Grimalkin playing with a wooden spool. Finally the spinning wheel stopped. The knitting needles lay idle in the girls' laps. The boys put their jackknives down. Even Grimalkin stopped his play.

"I feared it," said Papa, his face white.

"What is it?" asked Mamma in alarm.

"It is about Benjamin," Papa replied. "The letter comes from the Reverend Dr. Smith of the Academy at Philadelphia."

Benjamin's hands tightened around a handful of treenails until they dug into his flesh.

"Read it out," suggested Mamma.

Papa cleared his throat, then read very slowly.

"For
John West, Esquire
Door-Latch Inn
near Springfield
in Chester County

"*Dear Sr John West—I have this day seen a painting done by your son, Benjamin. It is a lively piece of work, and holds a promise for the future.*

"*I am desirous of schooling the lad in history. History needs painters. The printed word is sometimes cold. Pictures can set words on fire.*

"*As touching on the matter of money, I am of the belief that Benjamin can earn his keep and his schooling by painting miniatures.*

"*I hope you will approve my recommendation.*
"*I am,*
"*Yours most truly,*
William Smith
Provost, The Academy
Philadelphia"

Papa turned away from the fire and fixed his eyes on Benjamin. Something of the fire was left in his stare.

"I thought thee would outgrow painting," he said. "I thought it a childhood pastime like blindman's buff or puss-in-the-corner. I held great hopes for thee, lad. I never dreamed thee would become a painter of images."

"Then I can go?" asked Benjamin breathlessly.

"It is not for me to decide."

"For Mamma?"

"No. It is not a matter for Mamma to decide. It is for God. I will lay the whole matter before Him at the meetinghouse next First Day." In silence he raked ashes over the fire for the night and with a heavy step went upstairs to bed.

After his footsteps had died away, Grimalkin wrapped himself about Benjamin's boots and looked up questioningly.

"Don't forget *me* in thy plans," he seemed to say.

18. The Fate of Benjamin

THE days before the meeting were as cheerless as a hearth without a fire. Never once did Papa have to remind Benjamin to begin the day in silence. He began and ended it in silence. He had very little appetite. Every time he thought of the meeting he broke out in goose flesh.

Grimalkin, too, knew that something was amiss. He seldom purred. He refused to play. He would sit for hours, his paws tucked under him, his green eyes watching Benjamin.

When First Day came, Benjamin was ready for the meeting long before the family.

"Preened as glossy bright as a bird," Papa remarked kindly. "Boots clean. Face scrubbed and shining. Hair combed until the teeth marks of the comb lie like the furrows in a field."

Benjamin fidgeted with the buttons on his coat. He actually

wished Papa would think up a chore to make the time fly. It was Mamma, however, who came to the rescue.

"The day is sharp," she said. "The meetinghouse will be cold. Will thee prepare the foot warmers, son?"

Benjamin was glad of a task. He set the foot warmers on the floor. There were five of them—one for Mamma and each of the girls. He filled the little metal boxes with live coals from the fire, and clamped the lids down firmly. Then he had to scrub his hands all over again.

Now everyone was ready. Nanny Luddy stood waiting at the upping block.

Papa mounted. Thomas helped Mamma mount behind Papa. The rest of the family followed on foot. First came the boys according to their ages—John, Thomas, Samuel, Joseph and Benjamin. Then followed the girls—Sarah, Hannah, Mary and Elizabeth—carrying their foot warmers.

Benjamin glanced backward, hoping Grimalkin might come along. But Grimalkin was nowhere to be seen.

With a sigh, he fell into step. The snow crunched underfoot. Horsemen, their waistcoats flapping like bird wings, passed them

by. Sleighs filled with women and children passed them by, their runners squeaking above the wind. From the town of Goshen, from Springfield, from all over the countryside horses and oxen were climbing the long hill to the meetinghouse.

A cardinal flew across the road, his feathers blood-red against the snow-covered trees.

Just when Benjamin and his brothers reached the steps of the meetinghouse, a streak of black whisked by their feet. Seemingly from nowhere at all Grimalkin had come!

Waving his tail in the air, he walked directly to the men's section of the meetinghouse. In great dignity he found the bench where Benjamin always sat. He settled himself on the floor and politely waited.

No one paid him the slightest attention. Not even the two dogs on the women's side of the house who came along as foot warmers. They had tangled with Grimalkin in their puppyhood. Now they held him in great respect.

Mamma and Papa were already seated among the elders on a bench facing the congregation when Benjamin took his seat between Samuel and Joseph. A stilled, breathless feeling came over

him as he waited for the meeting to begin. From across the aisle came the rustle of skirts and the scraping of foot warmers being shoved into place.

Now everyone was settling down. The meeting was about to begin.

Usually Benjamin liked the silence of First Day. It seemed warm and friendly and comforting. Often it held a kind of power for him.

But today the silence was suffocating. It was like swimming underneath a bridge of logs and not being able to come up for air. The silence was growing deeper. It was a whirlpool now, sucking Benjamin down, down, down. He felt as if he were drowning in it.

Suddenly Papa was removing his hat. He rose with effort, as if for him the silence were a hand, trying to hold him down. He hung his hat on a peg in the wall behind him.

"Friends," he began so slowly that it was hard to piece the words together, "Friends—I have a grave matter to lay before the Society."

Then his words came more quickly.

"All children in Penn's colony should be taught a useful trade. It was William Penn's wish. I now seek guidance for my last-born son. He elects to be a painter."

Once more the silence closed in. Benjamin could hear Papa's breath coming and going. It sounded like a bellows.

If Papa had said, "My son elects to be a pirate," the stillness could not have been more fearful.

Benjamin rubbed his foot across Grimalkin's back. He saw little sparks fly.

"Since God has created beauty in nature, Benjamin sees no

sin in copying it," Papa explained. "I now lay the matter before Him. Shall Benjamin be called off from his painting?"

Again that heavy stillness, as Papa returned his hat to his head and sat down. The only sound Benjamin could hear was the wild beating of his heart.

Now, with a light scuffle of feet, a little man at the end of the row stood up. Benjamin took a sidewise glance at him. It was Beriah Hadwen, the wool comber from the town of Goshen. Benjamin never failed to marvel at the man's head. It was as bare as an opossum's tail.

"If I may so speak," said Mr. Hadwen, "it would seem best to call him off. Picturemaking belongs to the world and the things of the world." And with that he blew his nose and sat down.

At once a deep, pleasant voice was heard. It belonged to John Williamson, the ironmonger.

"Quakers," he was saying, "have given themselves the name of Friends. Are we being Friends in calling Benjamin off from his life's work?" He stopped and Grimalkin filled the gap with a loud purring. Mr. Williamson smiled. "Even Benjamin's cat, Grimalkin, was called upon to furnish paintbrushes for his master. So strong in Benjamin was the urge to reproduce God's work that he made his paintbrushes from his cat's fur. Determination is a good thing. We could all benefit."

Scarcely had he finished when Schoolmaster Snevely sprang up like a jack-in-the-box.

"I think it proper," he said, "that we name a committee of men and women to inspect Benjamin's pictures. It would be for them to decide whether Benjamin should be called off."

There was a stirring in the women's side of the meetinghouse as Mrs. Tomkins rose up, round as a haystack.

"I think it would be seemly," she bustled, "if we followed Master Snevely's advice. I name Schoolmaster Snevely to the committee."

Master Snevely bowed in her direction. "And I name Mrs. Tomkins."

The voices came thick and fast.

"I name Miller Clinkenbeard."

"I name Friend Williamson."

"I name Beriah Hadwen from Goshen."

"I name all of the elders."

"I name Dr. Jonathan Moris."

At last Mamma stood up.

"Next First Day afternoon," she said in her gentle voice, "I should like to invite the committee to Door-Latch Inn to inspect Benjamin's pictures and decide his fate." Only then did Mamma's blue eyes look to Papa for approval. He nodded solemnly.

And so it was.

19. The Latchstring Is In

Two days before the meeting, Papa took Benjamin completely by surprise. Except for Grimalkin and the cows, they were alone in the barn.

"Why doesn't thee get out thy paintbox?" Papa asked, as he aimed a stream of milk directly into Grimalkin's mouth.

"What for, Papa?"

"It would be nice to have a new signboard swinging from the buttonwood tree."

"But what is wrong with the sign there now?"

"The lettering is feeble," Papa replied. "A picture of a door-latch would be more fitting. It would say to wayfarers and journeymen: 'Welcome! The latchstring is out. Here thee will find food and lodging and comfort.' But mind thy colors," he added quickly. "Only grays or buffs. No bright gaudy tints."

125

As soon as the milking was done, Benjamin raced across the courtyard. He had not been so happy in days. He laughed out at Grimalkin, who bounded ahead of him like a snowshoe rabbit.

With a piece of hemp Benjamin took the measurements of the old weathered sign. Then he sawed some boards and set to work sanding them.

"I'll make two, three signs," he told Grimalkin. "It will keep me from thinking about things."

So Sixth Day and Seventh Day passed in a pleasant busyness.

First Day dawned bright and cold. The morning dragged. No one was moved to speak at meeting. The hour of worship seemed more like ten. But at last the family was home again, the noontide meal over, and the dishes back on their shelves.

An expectant feeling filled Door-Latch Inn. One could almost see it in the dancing flecks of winter sunlight, in the blue flames that licked the chimney.

Papa paced to and fro, with Grimalkin trying to catch his bootlaces. Mamma flew from room to room, giving out directions in a voice that did not hide her nervousness.

"Thee, Sarah, set up Benjamin's pictures in the parlor: the image of Sally on the table and that of Sassoonan and the Indians on the mantel shelf. No, try it the other way around. Aye, that is better. Now the cattail picture and the one of the flying squirrel can go on the mantel, too.

"Mary! Thee move the spinning wheel to the corner.

"Thee, Benjamin! Put bayberry candles in all the holders.

"Elizabeth! Thee's to cover the plate of caraway cakes with a white linen cloth. Then set the crock of whipped sillabub out in the snow to chill.

"Thomas and John! Be so good as to arrange the stools and chairs about the fire. Place them in small half-circles, so, and make two sections, as in the meetinghouse."

Suddenly Benjamin looked up the road. A whole procession of men and women on horses was moving downhill toward Door-Latch Inn. The black hats of the men and the bonnets of the women made sharp outlines against the clear winter sky.

"Oh!" groaned Benjamin, as he twisted the last candle into its holder.

The procession was coming closer now. He could hear the thud of horses' hoofs. Or was it the thumping of his heart?

All at once the inn was alive with bustle. Papa and the boys were running to help with the horses. Mamma and the girls were at the door, hanging cloaks and hoods on pegs, seeing to everyone's comfort. Everybody was stirring except Benjamin. He stood rooted to the floor. Grimalkin lay across his boots, his ears pointed backward with disapproval.

Time and again the door creaked open and shut, letting in black-cloaked figures.

At last every member of the committee had arrived: Schoolmaster Snevely, Mrs. Tomkins, Miller Clinkenbeard, Mr. Williamson, Dr. Moris, Beriah Hadwen from Goshen, and all of the elders.

They had to pass Benjamin to get into the parlor, and each, in turn, stopped to shake his hand and some had a word for Grimalkin. Benjamin's hands were hot and moist. Their hands felt cold and hard and dry. With a sinking heart, Benjamin noticed several elders shake their heads slowly.

Now Papa did something that Benjamin had never seen him do before. He shut the door securely and pulled the latchstring *inside*. As long as Benjamin could remember, the latchstring had always been out so that friend or stranger, Indian or white man, could lift the latch and walk in. Now no one else could enter.

Benjamin shuddered.

"Thee, Benjamin, may come into the parlor," said Papa.

20. The Fork in the Road

BENJAMIN stepped across the threshold. Little groups of people stood huddled about his pictures. Miller Clinkenbeard was running his finger along the painted cattails.

"Look mighty furry and natural," he chirped.

"La!" shrieked Mrs. Tomkins as she caught sight of the flying squirrel. "I thought the varmint was going to fly out of the picture and land in my hair. I can't abide flying creatures!" she whimpered, clapping her hands over her head.

After the committee had looked from picture to picture, they settled down like a flock of rusty blackbirds on a newly plowed field.

Papa motioned Benjamin to an empty stool in the front row

between Beriah Hadwen on the one side and Schoolmaster Snevely on the other. The elders sat on a long bench facing everyone else in the room.

Grimalkin now pattered softly down the narrow aisle between the women's and the men's sides, his ears laid back, his tail lashing the air. When he came to Beriah Hadwen, he stopped dead. The man was sitting on his favorite basket-bottom chair! Slowly he brought his four feet together and arched his back.

"*Ya-aeow-w!*" he spat, but only the family knew that he was trying to say, "Thee, stranger! Thee is sitting on my basket-bottom chair. It is mine! Mine! Mine!" Suddenly making a

spring, he seized the calf of Friend Hadwen's leg and began using it for a scratching post.

"Ee-ee!" screeched the wool comber, trying to shake Grimalkin off. But Grimalkin continued to sharpen his claws with great vigor on Friend Hadwen's wool stockings.

"Down!" whispered Benjamin in Grimalkin's ear, and the word was magic. Grimalkin stopped scratching and hid under the shadow of Benjamin's stool. A hush settled down over the parlor. It grew deeper. Benjamin watched the sands in the hourglass on the mantel. Seconds and minutes were spilling away.

At last he could feel a slight movement beside him. Schoolmaster Snevely was on his feet. His voice broke through the stillness.

"Life is a journey," he exclaimed in his schoolroom voice. "And sooner or later we come to a fork in the road. Benjamin faces the fork in his road. One way leads to Philadelphia and the occupation of painting; the other points to a useful trade. Aye," he sighed, "it is a grave concern that lies on this meeting. Let us now give due consideration to the matter."

In the silence that followed every head was bowed. All eyes were closed. Benjamin closed his eyes, too. Here in this room his future hung on a thread. A handful of grownups were going to decide about his whole life. How could they know that he was happy only when he painted? How could they know that to him nothing else seemed to matter?

He did not see Beriah Hadwen rise to his feet. He did not see Grimalkin spring upon the basket-bottom chair and settle down for a cat nap.

"Friends!" cheeped Beriah Hadwen in his birdlike voice, "pictures are ornaments and ornaments are needless. We have ever been a plain people. We need useful men: candlemakers and potters, and millers and sawyers, and, yes, wool combers. A man's *deeds* are fixed in the hearts of his friends. Not his fleshly image on a canvas."

And he sat down heavily on Grimalkin, as if the weight of his words were too much for him.

What a commotion! An ear-splitting howl from Grimalkin, and added to the howling came cries from Friend Hadwen, who shot into the air like an arrow from a blowgun.

"Poor kitling," soothed Benjamin, as he took Grimalkin in his arms. "Friend Hadwen did not know he was in thy favorite chair."

"The meeting can go forward," pronounced one of the elders as the room quieted down.

A long and uneasy silence followed. Benjamin wiped his moist hands on his breeches. The meeting seemed to be going forward, he thought, although no one was saying a word.

It was almost candlelighting time when a stool scraped across the floor in the men's section.

Benjamin said a quick prayer under his breath. Let it be Friend Williamson, O Lord. Let it be him.

"Friends!" the deep, pleasant voice of Mr. Williamson rang out. Thank Thee, O Lord, for Thy promptness, breathed Benjamin.

"Friends, journey back with me to the year 1682," the kindly voice was saying. "The good ship *Welcome* is sailing up the River Delaware. At her prow stands William Penn. His hand is resting on the shoulder of Thomas Pearson, the grandfather of our Benjamin West.

"Side by side these two men explore the very lands we now cultivate.

" 'What would *thee* name this spot of land?' asks William Penn of Friend Pearson.

" 'I would call it Chester,' replies Friend Pearson. And Chester it has been ever since."

Benjamin peered around at the committee. Black hats and starched white caps were nodding in agreement.

"Now skip the years with me," Mr. Williams was saying. "William Penn is dead. Friend Pearson is dead. But we, their children, carry on. Mrs. West, Friend Pearson's own daughter, is here among us. She and John West have raised ten children. Many of us can call to mind the miracle of Benjamin's birth."

Benjamin could almost feel his ears prick forward. What was this about a miracle? What was this?

"It was a First Day morning of autumn, in the year 1738," Mr. Williamson's voice rolled on. "The great preacher, Edmond Peckover, was visiting Chester County. He preached in our meetinghouse until the very rafters seemed lighted with an Inner Light.

"So deeply was Mrs. West stirred that her tenth child, Benjamin, was born before his time. Thee, Dr. Moris, will remember Edmond Peckover's words."

"Aye," agreed Dr. Moris, "I remember them well. '*Thy son will be no ordinary man,*' he predicted, as he shook Mr. West's hand."

Benjamin grew wide-eyed. Why, how very exciting! he thought. He had never heard this story before. He looked across at Mamma. Her hands were folded quietly, and she looked into the fire as if there the whole story were repeated.

Mr. Williamson took a deep breath. "Edmond Peckover's words have come to pass," he said. "God has given a great gift to Benjamin—the art of painting. Who can say that it shall be quenched like fire? Let him use this gift to portray the best that is in Nature and in Man. If I may so say, the signpost on his road points to Philadelphia."

Suddenly voices were raised from every part of the room.

"I hold with Friend Williamson's words."

"I hope the committee will approve his words."

"I am of the same mind."

"Yea."

"Yea."

"Yea."

Schoolmaster Snevely rose. "A boy who found his colors in the earth, who made his own brushes from his cat's tail, who used poplar boards for paper—such a boy should be sent to Philadelphia with our blessings."

"We are all in agreement," piped the wool comber from Goshen, but this time he did not rise from his basket-bottom chair.

A short period of silence followed, a warm, friendly silence. It made Benjamin feel good to the very soles of his feet.

Now the elders turned to one another, shook hands, and suddenly the meeting was over. Somehow, Papa's and Mamma's and Benjamin's eyes met. There was a smile among them.

Then Papa stirred the fire and Mamma lighted the bayberry candles. Never before had the parlor seemed so bright. Firelight danced on the walls and gave color to the sober faces of the elders. The candles burned yellow arrows of light and held them in soft blue halos.

Benjamin was the center of a buzzing circle. How nice their hands feel! he thought. Not hard and cold at all, but warm and rough, like Grimalkin's tongue.

As the circle widened, there was a little lull. It was plain to see that everyone expected Benjamin to say something. For a long time no sound came—only the singing of the fire.

"I aim to make you glad of your belief in me," Benjamin said at last. "I aim to make you glad."

"Friends," Mamma announced from the doorway, "a little refreshment is ready."

Not counting the family, twenty-six sat down to table. Everyone was in fine appetite. The whipped sillabub vanished like snow in April, and the mountain of caraway cakes dwindled until only a few crumbs were left.

The sky was hanging out its flickering lanthorns when the committee members mounted their horses and turned out of the courtyard. Grimalkin chased them until they were well beyond the gate. Then he flew back into the house and tucked his snow-wet paw into Benjamin's hand. He held it there for a very long time, as much as to say, "I congratulate thee, too, Benjamin, but don't forget me in thy plans."

21. The Unknown Journeyman

Two mornings later Benjamin stood in the center of the kitchen, wondering what to do with himself. It seemed strange to be wearing his First Day suit on Third Day. He had never noticed it before, but his arms were too long for the sleeves. He felt as gangly as a newborn colt!

His eyes glanced about the kitchen and fell upon his knapsack. For two days now it had leaned against the wall like a tired person.

Grimalkin slept on it by the hour. It was as if he knew it held all of Benjamin's belongings as well as his own things—the collar and lead that Benjamin had made for him in Philadelphia, a packet of dried catmint, the bell he always wore around his neck during the bird-nesting season, his wooden dinner basin.

"Is thee below, Benjamin?" called Mamma from the head of the stairway. "The girls are tidying thy room," she said with a catch in her voice. "They found this poplar board behind thy bed."

Slowly she made her way down the stairway, treasuring the poplar board as if it had been a lock of hair.

"Methinks some journeyman bound for Philadelphia will surely come today," she said. "The snow is stopped. The hollows in the road are well packed for travel. The streams are frozen and passable. Sleighing will be exceedingly pleasant."

Benjamin was a long time answering. He knew he should be happy, but somehow the kitchen was warm and cozy and Philadelphia seemed big and far away. And the very thought of traveling with an unknown journeyman made him break out in prickles of goose flesh. Suppose the man was not overfond of cats. Suppose . . .

Mamma seemed to read Benjamin's mind. "A mannerly cat is welcome even on a journey," she replied with firm assurance. "And when the stranger sees the good bean porridge all frozen in a solid chunk and ready to tie onto his sleigh, he will be glad of a boy and a cat for company. Thee had best take a hatchet along to chop the porridge.

"Now then," Mamma went on with a little smile, "it has been in my mind a pretty while that we have no image of Grimalkin, except the one in our hearts. I desire a good likeness to set upon the mantel. Begin it now, lad, whilst I draw my bread from the oven."

Benjamin tried to speak, but a choking filled his throat. How nice it was that he and Mamma did not need words!

He lifted the knapsack with Grimalkin still dozing on it, and moved it to a little patch of sunlight. The cat stretched, opened a sleepy eye, and watched with grave interest. Then he yawned a long pink yawn and gazed up with an air of approval that said quite plainly, "This now, *this* is like olden times!"

Benjamin's paintbox was packed away in the knapsack, so he began rummaging in the little cubbyhole beside the hearth. He found a small hard lump of yellow clay, softened it with skimmed milk, and added some indigo from the dye pot. "This be as green as thy eyes," he said to Grimalkin as he stirred the mixture. Then he picked up a piece of charcoal and set to work. Oh, the joy of having something to do! "If I don't watch myself, I might purr like Grimalkin," he laughed.

His hands moved swiftly and surely. And little by little the whiskery face of a cat began to look out from the poplar board. It was an impish face. Ears pricked forward. Mouth open in a mischievous smile. Eyes green and shining.

Benjamin was lost in a world of his own. He did not hear the clicking of the latch. He did not hear the door creak open and then shut again. He did not feel the cold gust of wind that swirled into the room.

Suddenly a hand gripped his shoulder and a voice whispered in awe, "Iss Grimalkin you paint?"

Benjamin almost fell off his stool. He whirled around and stood facing a tall blond boy, a boy whose sleeves were too short for his jacket.

"Jacob! Jacob Ditzler! It is thee!" And then his tongue went silent.

Jacob's eyes were fastened on Grimalkin. Moving slowly now, so as not to frighten the cat, he walked around Benjamin and stopped before the knapsack.

Grimalkin leaped lightly to the floor and began sniffing Jacob's boots. Then he rubbed himself against Jacob's legs. In an instant Jacob was on his knees, his arms around Grimalkin. "Ai! Yai! Yai!" he breathed. "You don't forget Jacob. It wonders me how you remember." At last he turned to Benjamin, his eyes filled with happiness. "Chust like you said. A house cat you make of him. You here right along, ain't?"

"No, Jacob, I'm going to Philadelphia—to paint. Think on it. To *paint!*"

"No!" exclaimed Jacob. "Ach, no!"

Benjamin nodded.

"Why, I go, too, Benjamin. My pa iss out in the wagon shed mit your pa. A new sleigh we got and *two* oxen already. We go by Philadelphia too. Soon a shipbuilder I am. Soon I make ropes and sails. . . . Ach, Benjamin, you can ride to Philadelphia along, ain't?"

Suddenly Door-Latch Inn rang with noise and laughter. The girls flew downstairs from their cleaning. Papa and the boys and Mr. Ditzler came in, stamping the snow from their feet.

The kettle was singing over the fire. The table board was heaped with hot corn bread and deermeat and cheese and eggs and blueberry tarts.

But Benjamin and Jacob were so full of plans they had little room for food. Besides, they were looking forward to building a fire in Penn's forest together and chopping off a great hunk of frozen bean porridge and heating it over their own fire.

Mr. Ditzler, however, had a robust appetite. He cleaned his plate three times. Then he looked out at the sky.

"Chust midday," he announced as he wiped his mouth on his sleeve. "If ve go now ve get maybe ten, twelf miles behind us already before dark night comes."

In a moment the entire family was standing before a bright red sleigh in the winter sunshine of the courtyard. Everything was in readiness—Benjamin's knapsack wedged in between a little cowhide trunk of Jacob's and a bag of feed for the oxen, the bean porridge tied onto the back of the sleigh. Now Mr. Ditzler and Jacob and Benjamin climbed in the sleigh and let Mamma and Papa tuck them in snugly with a bearskin.

"My little wren," whispered Mamma while Papa scowled and grunted to hide his real feelings.

Grimalkin leaped up on Benjamin's shoulder and placed one paw on Jacob's back. He sniffed Jacob in a warm friendly way, playfully cuffing the tail of his foxskin cap.

"Gee-op!" cried Mr. Ditzler.

Slowly, the oxen shuffled off, their sleigh bells playing a kind of haunting tune.

When Door-Latch Inn was out of sight Jacob turned to Benjamin with a deep sigh. "Everything gets all right, ya?"

"Aye, *everything*," chuckled Benjamin.

And Grimalkin let out a happy *purr-r-r-rieu* into the frosty air.

D.

22. Father of American Painting

IT WAS a morning, clear and joyous, in the summer of 1898. Nearly one hundred and fifty years had passed since the little red sleigh set out for Philadelphia.

Knots of people were gathering about an old stone house in Swarthmore, Pennsylvania. An American flag veiled the space between two windows of the house. It stirred lightly with the wind, but gave no hint of what was underneath.

For several hours the crowds kept on coming—in surreys and gigs and high spring wagons. Men in tan derby hats stroked their chin whiskers and pulled out from their vest pockets enormous gold watches on long chains. Ladies in tiny black bonnets and long silk skirts rustled their children into a little half-circle about the flag.

As the morning wore on, sun parasols popped out, thick as mushrooms after a rain.

At last a man with a trim white beard took his place before the flag.

"It's the Reverend Mr. Joseph Vance," the word went around.

Voices quieted. An expectant hush settled down over the wide green lawn.

"Friends," came the deep-toned voice of the Reverend Mr. Vance, "we are gathered here to keep green the memory of Benjamin West. One hundred and sixty years ago he was born in the south room of this house."*

And while the bees played an obbligato and a wren sputtered at the disturbance, Mr. Vance began to draw little pictures in everyone's mind. He showed the boy, Benjamin, making a "hair pencil" from the fur of his cat's tail. He showed him with the Indians, digging his colors from the earth. He showed him standing, trembling and fearful, before the elders and overseers, hoping they would not "call him off from his painting." He showed him studying history at the Academy of Philadelphia and painting miniatures to earn his keep.

Then he transported his hearers across the ocean where Benjamin West became President of the Royal Academy of England, and court painter to His Majesty George III, King of Great Britain and Ireland.

"Friends!" said Mr. Vance as he measured his words with slow

---

*The house is still standing. It may be seen on the campus of Swarthmore College, at Swarthmore, Pennsylvania.

purpose. "It was Benjamin West who first dared to paint historical figures as they actually appeared—Indians in their war paint, British officers in their scarlet coats. Other artists of his day held to the old custom of clothing all historical figures in long white mantles called *togas*."

A slow smile spread over Mr. Vance's face. "I like to picture Benjamin West wearing his Quaker hat in Windsor Palace and refusing a knighthood because, as he himself told the King, 'To Quakers, titles are needless. The only title we covet is that of Friend.'"

When at last the Reverend Mr. Vance folded his paper and slipped it into its envelope, W. Benjamin West, a descendant of Benjamin's brother Samuel, stepped up to the flag. With trembling fingers he drew a cord. The flag rose. And there, placed in the stone of the wall, was a memorial tablet. He read the inscription

BENJAMIN WEST,
PRESIDENT OF THE
ROYAL ACADEMY -
WAS BORN IN THIS HOUSE
8TH MONTH, 10, 1738
o
PLACED BY THE DELAWARE
COUNTY HISTORICAL SOCIETY

in a clear voice so that it carried to the very outer fringe of the gathering.

In the quiet that followed, the boys and girls began to sing "The Star-Spangled Banner." Their voices were high and thin at first, but as the grownups joined in, the notes swelled until they carried as far as the little community of Westdale, named for Benjamin West.

Long seconds after the last note had been sung, the crowd stood still. They had journeyed so far back into America that they were a long time returning. Slowly the sun umbrellas clicked shut. Slowly the people walked back to their horses. They still seemed part of the long ago and the far away. They had struggled with the boy Benjamin, as he overcame great odds. They had watched the boy grow until he became the father of American painting.

It was not easy for them to begin talking in their everyday voices, as if nothing had happened to them. Something *had* happened to them. They had gone a-leafing and found a page of American history.

A Note of Acknowledgment

FOR THEIR HELP THE AUTHOR IS GRATEFUL TO

Elsie M. Jones, Curator, Delaware County Historical Society, Chester, Pennsylvania

Theodore Sizer, Director, Yale University Art Gallery

Richard D. Buck, Acting Head, Department of Conservation, Harvard University, Fogg Museum of Art

Meyric R. Rogers, Curator of Decorative Arts and Industrial Arts, Chicago Art Institute

Ruth Butler, Custodian, Edward E. Ayer Collection of North and South American Indians, Newberry Library, Chicago, Illinois

Sykes Hartin, Reference Department, The Library of Swarthmore College, Swarthmore, Pennsylvania

H. H. Hewitt and Roberta Sutton, Chicago Public Library

Marjorie G. Wright, Aurora Public Library

Grace Luenzmann, Wayne, Illinois

147